The Moralist

*A Tale of People and Events in Centerfield,
Texas, during a Year Recently Concluded*

The Moralist

A Tale of People and Events in Centerfield, Texas,
during a Year Recently Concluded

By John Warley

To Lorie & George, host and hostess without peer, with heartfelt thanks for Beach Week 2018.

Dedication

To my valued early readers and supporters in Newport News, Virginia, whose encouragement meant so such, then and now:

Janice Harvey

Betsy J. Miller

Doug & Tadd Chessen

Charlene S. Smyth

Chapter 1

Our Lady of the Lease Appears to George in a Vision

George Fafalone, lying in a hospital bed, floated above it on a cushion of morphine, his nose intubated and consciousness just beyond reach. Keeping guard over his post-op recovery, digital sentries bleeped, buzzed and hummed in their twenty-first century argot, turning the air around him a glowing, kryptonite green. Somewhere in the distance he thought he heard laughter, and it roused him. He opened one eye.

The clock on the wall showed 8:10 — a.m.? He thought of how lucky he was to still be alive, and of how, if it was a.m., the stock market would open in twenty minutes. He usually relied on his watch, a Rolex, but of course they would have removed it prior to surgery, and he was anxious to see his wife, for he felt certain the triage nurse would have given it to her for safekeeping. He opened the other eye. Laughter down the hall grew. Shift change, he speculated through a narcotic haze. He owed his life to a spirited response by the EMS team and to his heart surgeon, Dr. Tan. A close one, he acknowledged. Then, he closed his eyes, and they remained closed even after he felt pressure on his right hand, a compelling squeeze he attributed to his wife. At any moment, she would bend down to kiss him chastely, surgically on the cheek, careful to avoid contact with the various hoses, lines and machines surrounding him. He waited. It wasn't every day a man suffered his first heart attack, so he might as well milk it. He didn't return the squeeze, and he didn't open his eyes. Lying there, seemingly comatose, he waited for the kiss and reminded himself to ask about his Rolex.

Instead, he heard a voice, close to his right ear, and it was not the voice of Joyce, his wife.

"George," it said, "George Fafalone." The voice, female, registered as chummy, almost intimate, and the tiny puff of air against his cheek carried a scent that was not Joyce's. He opened his eyes to see Fran, his neighbor and the tenant of his rental house next door.

I'm hallucinating, he told himself.

"Hi, George," she said, friendly enough. "I heard."

He tried to speak but she moved her hand gently to his mouth.

"Don't talk," she said. "You've had a very tough time. I saw your wife this morning. She said you were doing fine. Are you in pain? Blink once for yes and twice for no."

He blinked twice, then tried to lift his hand against the absurdity of such a dream as the one he must be in.

"You may be wondering why I'm here," Fran said. "You're probably asking yourself, 'what is on Fran's mind that won't wait until I get home from this near-death adventure?' Is that what you're thinking? Blink once for yes and twice for no." George blinked once. She moved closer, bending down toward him. "It's the sink, George. It's stopped up again, and I can't wash dishes and I can't cook. Remember? We talked about it last weekend, and you were going to send the plumber. Did you call him, because if you did he never came, just like last time when the pipe broke. It's not easy to feed three children when the sink is broken."

George thought he heard more laughter from the nurses' station. He considered yelling.

"Okay, I'll confess," said Fran, who was slim, about forty, not pretty but pleasant, with little upturned creases at her eyes that influenced her entire face. She wore no makeup. "It's not just the sink, or the lock on the side door, or the window in the back that has been broken since last summer. I've had some other thoughts I wanted to share with you. This seems like as good a time as any because you're not an easy landlord to get hold of, even though you live next door. Am I right there, George? Remember? I came over while you were pulling out of the driveway and you powered down the window long enough to say you had some big meeting you needed to make even though it was Saturday and you looked like you were dressed for golf. You were going to call me right after the meeting and maybe it's my phone but I don't think you did and I've left all those messages and well, I just never seem to be able to reach you when there's a problem."

2

He opened his mouth but no words came and she again moved her hand to quiet him.

"So, the big one, eh? Who could have predicted it? Answer: just about anyone with two functioning brain cells. Look at you— 325 pounds of sweaty success." She fingered the IV suspended above his bed. "This liquid diet must be hard on your system. By the time you leave here, you'll be good and ready for those three-egg omelets, the bacon, the gravy biscuits, the hash browns, deep fried of course." She smiled, her voice still even and non-threatening. Then, without breaking eye contact, she braced herself on the bed frame, climbed onto the bed, brought her right leg deftly over him and straddled his stomach as if to copulate with his navel. He wondered if her knees rested on his oxygen tube. Leaning close, her nose almost touching his, she said in a voice still calm, yet firm: "Because we're neighbors, I see more of you than I want to. And after watching you for the past year, I've come to some conclusions. Want to hear them? I thought so. You're an utter moron. You're a flaccid, gluttonous, consumptive moron, who probably won't live much longer—certainly not long enough to fix my sink or the window in the back—but if you ever get on your feet again, you really ought to try exercise once in a while, and not just sitting in a golf cart or hoisting those vodka martinis but some real exercise. And push away from the table every now and then. It won't kill you? Get it? That's called irony."

Fran leaned back, brought her hands to his ears, grabbed the thinning hair at the temples and pulled his head forward, her voice rising. "Look at me. I'm raising three kids in that dump we rent from you and I still find time to exercise four times a week. Do I look fat to you? Hell no, because I don't eat enough for three every time I sit down. You know, George, I'll probably live to be a hundred, maybe more with all this stuff." She released one clump of hair long enough to wave her arm, encompassing the room's digital readout apparatus. His head listed to one side. "You? I don't give you six months. Of course, I could get hit by a bus, we're all vulnerable to that, but if I don't I'll be walking over your grave for four or five decades." She released her grip. His head sank back into the pillow as she swung her leg over him and dismounted. "Okay, I've had my say. Just remember, all this stuff you're

3

plugged into costs big bucks, and if your insurance company didn't have to pay so much to keep buffet bandits like you going, maybe it could find a way to cover me and my kids. I really don't want to pay to keep you alive any longer than it takes to get my sink fixed — no offense. Before I shell out my hard-earned money to perform modern miracles on your wasted excuse for a body, you ought to try harder yourself. I guess what I'm saying, George, is that you're just taking up space, not to mention a repulsive amount of food. I'll be home all week if the plumber needs to get in."

George resolved to speak with Dr. Tan about changing his medication.

4

Chapter 2

We Meet the Family Fafalone

George survived. He went home one week after his attack, and when Joyce drove into their driveway he looked at Fran's. "I need to get a plumber over there," he said.

George and Joyce lived in 10,000 square feet of modern affluence, space they were considering expanding now that Kirstin was on her own and Scott was thinking about college. The house next door, Fran's rental, had been their starter home years ago. Both George and Joyce had been happier there, but neither admitted it and upon moving Joyce had planted a bank of slow-growing shrubs that would one day complete the separation between their old happiness and their new success.

Like nearly all Centerfield residents, George came from somewhere else. He and Joyce had married in Los Angeles and moved to Texas twenty-five years before. For a month after their arrival he surveyed possible business opportunities before settling for one he considered a slam dunk winner: death. He started the town's first and only funeral home. His company had expanded with Centerfield's population and now employed twelve people, all men except for a cupcake receptionist named Joanie. The company's motto had been controversial since Day 1: "We're here when you're not." George himself had come up with this bon mote and was quite proud of it, suggesting to those who deemed it tasteless that denying death was futile and embracing death, as did Fafalone Eternal Enterprises, LLC, was what set his company apart. Besides, he reminded them, the nearest competitor in Houston was twice as expensive, employed non-certified embalmers, and hired ex-cons to drive inferior hearses. George modeled the business along the lines of used cars, which had in fact been his business in LA. His new TV ad featured Joanie in a low-cut blouse, prancing around the showroom to tout the latest models like they were automobiles. "And over here," she cloyed in breathy Marilynesque

5

tones, "we have the Divine Deliverer, certain to grab the attention of those you leave behind and the one you are getting ready to meet. And remember, on-the-spot financing is always available at Fafalone's Temple of Repose." She loved doing the commercials so much that she rarely asked for a raise, and only gave out with demure little giggles when George fondled her during the Christmas party. George also owned the cemetery ("serious money" he confided to his poker club). Economically, Centerfield boomed. It had gone from a zip code to a city in twenty years, and virtually everyone who died made their last purchase from George.

George and Joyce bought new cars every other year, a Lexus for him and an Escalade for her. A Mercedes lounged in the garage as a spare. They vacationed in the same house in Deer Isle, Maine, for three weeks every August, had sex twice a year not counting the time in Maine, split their ticket when they voted, spoke often of the "wolf at the door," religiously checked the performance of their mutual funds and IRAs, and had begun to ponder whether, in order to live on a golf course in their retirement, Joyce should take up golf.

As insurance against whatever awaited them in the hereafter, they had joined a mega-church in Houston, to which Joyce drove weekly and George and Joyce together drove quarterly. Each had their respective passions. For Joyce, it was celebrity awards shows and any charity endorsed by Sean Penn ("His compassion is so . . . compassionate"). For George, it was illegal immigration, and while his company employed five undocumented Mexicans (gravediggers) and his household another three, he ranted about porous borders and had recently made a major donation to a secret right-wing group committed to installing land mines along both sides of an electrically charged fence running the entire length of US-Mexico border.

They considered Scott a "difficult kid," a phrase they had also applied to Kirstin until she moved out. One August in Maine, George had suggested that Kirstin lacked morals, and as her parents, they had to take some responsibility for this shortcoming. Joyce disagreed, insisting they had done all they could and that kids today were faced with what she called "tough problems."

George's doubts about Kirstin, however, forced Joyce to try some new things with Scott. For example, she recommended movies that she had enjoyed and which carried the double benefits of entertainment and instruction. She announced what she called her "video rule" — for each slasher movie Scott ordered, he agreed to watch one "wholesome" movie from a list she drew up and posted on the refrigerator door. The list, some thirty-five titles in all, included two Muppet films, which Joyce believed promoted a theme of loyalty, as well as *The Witches of Eastwick*, which she conceded was not particularly wholesome, but she had always been a Jack Nicholson fan. She took pride in this parental innovation, while Scott pronounced it "dumber than frog shit," a phrase that always made Joyce laugh and remind Scott that wit like his could take him far in the world. The voice of Joyce said, "Jay Leno can't go on forever."

Scott tolerated the video rule because he had seen the Muppet movies when he was four and never watched the others, crossing them off the refrigerator list without hesitation. Joyce suspected that her system contained potential for abuse, and debated with herself the wisdom of verifying Scott's compliance. On one hand, she had heard somewhere that trust was a key ingredient of the parent-child relationship, and on the other she had seen an afternoon talk show which championed "tough love" as a useful tool for tough problems. In the spirit of the talk show, she confronted him one afternoon with a pop quiz of sorts. "If you watched the video," she asked, pointing to a title he had just scratched through, "what happens at the end in *Love Story*?" When he hesitated, she recalled how she had cried when Ryan O'Neil left the hospital and how beautiful Allie McGraw looked in spite of everything and how no one had ever made a movie which better illustrated the truth, that life was beautiful if fragile and not always fair. "She died," guessed Scott.

Also, the much ridiculed video rule did not infringe on the use of his computer, at which he spent an increasing number of hours. When he was thirteen, he had spent an equal number of hours in the bathroom exploring his newly arrived manhood, and it was during that period that he had logged on to the internet in what began as a sincere effort to determine whether it was normal for

7

him to feel such an attraction to women's orthopedic shoes. He soon determined that his affinity was called a fetish in medical jargon, that fetishes came in all shapes and sizes to all economic and social groupings, that what sounded strange to some could actually prove quite harmless, even liberating to others, and that they did not require intense psychotherapy unless accompanied by violent or aberrational antisocial behavior, none of which he was experiencing at that time. In fact, the sole manifestation of his fetish that might have been considered antisocial was his pilfering from the school library the magazine *Elegant Elders*, a *GQ* for seniors, which predictably displayed pictures of older women in orthopedic shoes, as did a catalog he had found for durable medical equipment. He kept the catalog in the bathroom.

Scott felt some relief after learning that fetishes were common and medically substantiated. Nevertheless, he sensed isolation with his particular fetish as he scoured the internet for soul mates. He found chat rooms with spirited participation on the subjects of men's and women's underwear, body odors, chains and collars, intimate tattoos, and innovative uses for shaving creams. He browsed photographic displays of men with women, women with women, women with dogs, men with goats, and even dogs with sheep. These bored and frustrated him, and he began to despair. "I'm weird," he concluded. He decided to approach his mother, but he could not bring himself to disclose exactly what it was that excited him, so he referred somewhat vaguely to "strange feelings." Joyce listened patiently for over a minute, then recommended he watch *Thelma and Louise*, as she recalled that strange feelings had been one of its themes.

Scott was now seventeen, and about this time, just after George's heart attack, the voice of Joyce said, "I'm worried about Kirstin."

George looked up from his brokerage statement. "Why, dear?"

"I think she may be pregnant again. I didn't want to tell you until your heart was better."

"Are you sure?"

"No, not positive. Just a mother's instinct. She gets very moody when this happens. She was really down when I called to see if she was going to visit you in the hospital. Maybe you should talk to her."

"Me? What can I say I haven't said already? You're a woman, you talk to her."

"I can't. We're too close."

"Well, someone has to talk to her," said George. "She can't just get herself knocked up every six months. Whatever happened to birth control?"

"Oh, George, you make it sound so vulgar. Maybe Father Richards should speak to her."

"I have a better idea. What about Fran?"

"Fran who?" the voice of Joyce asked.

"Fran our next door neighbor. Our tenant."

"What business is it of hers?"

George related his confrontation in the ICU.

"Why, that crazy bitch," Joyce said. "She could have killed you. We should have her arrested for assault or something."

"I thought about it, but there is one small problem—I'm not absolutely sure it happened. I'd been hitting that morphine pump pretty hard; it could have been the drugs. But if it did happen, she's one lady who can speak her mind. Her kids seem nice. Maybe she would talk to Kirstin."

"George, that's a nutzo idea. She doesn't even *know* Kirstin. How can she relate? Kirstin isn't going to talk to some stranger about her problems."

"Like she's going to open up to Father Richards?"

Joyce admitted he had a point.

"I'll speak to Fran," he said. "I have to check on the sink anyway."

Chapter 3

George Gulps Pride and Lemonade

George walked next door, where Fran's son Chip clipped a hedge. He paused to catch his breath. "Your Mom at home?" he asked, winded.

"Yes, sir, she's inside," said Chip.

George hesitated at the front door. His blistering at the hospital, if she really had appeared at the hospital, remained fresh in his mind. And if she hadn't appeared, if the entire episode had been nothing more than a bad, one act skit in his sedated brain, wasn't it possible that some inner truth had availed itself of the chance to pounce on him as surely as he recalled Fran having done? The messenger, whether Fran or morphine, had overstated his shortcomings, no doubt, and failed to credit him with employing people and stimulating the economy with spending and, in the old days, buying brooms from the Lions Club, plus other worthiness he could think of if he had more time. He knocked.

Fran answered the door. "Come in," she said. "How are you feeling?"

George stepped inside. "Much better than the last time you saw me." He studied her for signs of sheepishness.

"Good. Have a seat."

Seeing no sheep, he said, "Ah, when *was* the last time you saw me?"

"What do you mean?" Fran asked.

"Well, was it in the driveway that day when you asked about the plumber . . . or later, in the hospital?"

"I came to the hospital."

"Of course you did," George said, nodding his head. "So we talked, at the hospital."

"I talked, you listened," Fran said, seemingly unfazed.

George stared down at the floor. "That was a gutsy thing you did, coming to see me like that."

10

"I needed the sink fixed," she said.

"And is it fixed?"

"The plumber came Monday morning. It seems to be working. Thank you. Would you like some lemonade? It's fresh."

"Yes, I would."

Fran walked to the kitchen and returned with lemonade. "Something on your mind?"

"My daughter, Kirstin."

"She must not live with you," Fran said. "I've never seen her."

"She moved out before you got here. She went to live with her boyfriend, then they broke up and she moved into her own place at The Crossing."

"Nice address. She must have a good job."

"She's studying manicure. I'm helping her out with the expense. Hey, she's my only daughter."

"Why are you coming to me?"

"Kirstin has some lifestyle issues. I thought maybe you could talk to her, being a mother and all."

"What about her own mother?"

"Joyce says they're too close, but between you and me that is not exactly the case. You know that mother-daughter thing. They don't get along so well right now, and Joyce has a hard time relating to Kirstin's problems."

"I see."

"I was thinking that you could make an appointment at Kirstin's school. I'd pay for it, of course. While she was doing your nails, you could get to know her."

"I don't think so. If she comes to see me, I'll speak with her, but it would be wrong for me to seek her out that way."

"You sought me out. Did you ever."

"You're my landlord. I had a reason."

"But you'll talk to her?"

"I'll speak with her, as I said."

"Good. Joyce will be so relieved. Me too. And hey, I'm gonna lose weight. You'll see." George laughed nervously.

"That would be wise," Fran said.

Chapter 4

A Name in Name Only

From the time of its founding in 1898, the town that would become Centerfield had been known by the inspirational name "Twig," a place that owed its existence to a single oil rig that gushed, briefly, at the close of the century. Twig served as the county seat for Bucko County, part of a rural Outback beginning fifty miles from Houston. The county consisted of vast areas of vast area, largely unexplored and only sparsely inhabited by some cattle, hearty sheep, and a few people. Ninety-eight percent of Bucko's population resided in Twig, which marked its eastern-most boundary. The citizens of Twig viewed Houston as a cousin once or twice removed, distantly blood related but from the oddball side of the Texas family and in any event endurable for the one or two times a year they needed to travel there.

Then came the reign of King Lyndon and Queen Space, showering federal largess at Houston in the form of petro-dollars and space shuttle cost overruns. A mushroom-shaped cloud of high rise buildings could be felt if not seen all the way to Twig, whose residents watched in horror for a decade as the cloud rose and an aftershock of asphalt approached. What must have been an army of urban planners and highway engineers in Houston planned ever more elaborate traffic arteries, with flyovers and HOV lanes and exit ramps plainly visible from the space shuttles that, like those same roads and bridges, were being controlled in Houston. By contrast, the road between Houston and Twig (with some logic known as Branch Road) was unpaved until 1955, and while there was grudging agreement among the citizens of Twig that the paving had reduced the dust for those annual or semiannual trips to Houston, the one urban planner in Twig, who was also the part-time sheriff, spent his time plotting to convert Branch Road to a toll road, the toll payable by anyone without Bucko County tags. The legal border between Twig and its urban cousin was San Pedro

Creek, an arroyo that was dry 10 months a year. For the good citizens of Twig, the creek might as well have been the Rio Grande.

All that began to change in 1978, when the Houston Astros signed a young Mexican phenom named Antonio Federico Macondo Bustamonte, affectionately known as Buster by Astros faithful. With his signing bonus, Buster bought a ranch and built a hacienda in Twig. Included in the purchase was the lone oil rig. He made the All-Star team at first base eleven years running, hit over .335 for nine consecutive seasons, and retired at age thirty-five, elected to the Baseball Hall of Fame in his first year of eligibility. The fans in Houston loved him, but the residents of his adopted "village," as he called it, venerated him. Every year the citizens of Twig gathered under the window of his hacienda to sing "Deep in the Heart of Texas" as Buster beamed from above. When the song ended, he would give his trademark swoosh, a way he had of catching a ball at first base and gracefully continuing the ball's momentum by extending his gloved hand to full reach. It was a gesture he had learned from watching bullfights in his native San Miguel de Allende and mirrored the sweep of the cape made by the matador as the bull's horn passed within inches of the groin. Once the swoosh had been performed with Buster's predictable finesse, he would be joined on the balcony by his wife Carlotta and their five children. As the children grew, the balcony had to be expanded, but this was of small concern since Buster was by then one of the highest paid players in the game.

So adored were Buster and his family that it was resolved to re-name the town for him. Except for the toll road proposal, this caused the first political crisis in Twig's history. None of its residents much wanted to live in a place called "Buster," least of all its homophobic mayor. Nor did the "City of Bustamonte" hold any appeal. "Antonio" would be confused with San Antonio and "Federico" with Frederick. "Macondo" suited no one, both because it was an obscure name not popularly associated with the great Buster and because the school librarian thought that such a name would be seen as a feeble imitation of the South American city that had endured one hundred years of solitude.

13

"We can't call it 'First Base'," the mayor opined. "We'll be the butt of endless jokes about people not being able to get to First Base."

"He played center field before they moved him to first base," someone recalled. "We could name our town Centerfield." It resonated, Buster approved, and it was done.

Chapter 5

Lenny Leaves Lenore as Kirstin's Credit Card is Declined

Joyce was watching a soap opera when Kirsten and Pete came roaring up the driveway on Pete's Harley. They entered the house without knocking. Pete diverted to the kitchen for a beer while Kirsten sought her mother in the den. Joyce batted the air for silence as her daughter entered.

"Hold a second, hon," Joyce said without taking her eyes from the 50 inch plasma screen. "Lenny is about to tell Lenore that he's leaving her. I had a feeling this might happen. It serves Lenore right because she is pure trash." From the tube came Lenny's melodramatic pronouncement.

"Lenore, we've grown apart. This will hurt, but there is someone else who completes me."

Lenore: "Oh Lenny, I knew something wasn't right. Is it Samantha?"

Lenny, looking down: "No, it's not Samantha."

Lenore: "Don't tell me it's Carla?"

Lenny, looking up: "Who is Carla?"

Lenore: "My tennis partner at the club. So it's not Carla?"

Lenny, locked in riveting eye contact: "It's Stuart."

Lenore: "But Stuart's so . . ."

Lenny, smiling faintly: "Young? Yes, twenty-two. Can you believe it?"

Lenore, heroically with clinched fists beating on Lenny's chest: "I won't give you up without a fight!"

Joyce nodded triumphantly as a dish detergent filled the screen. "Did I call it? Did I? You were here when I predicted it. Please remember to tell your father because sometimes I think he doesn't give me enough credit."

15

Kirstin parked her gum to one side of her jaw and said, "Speaking of credit, can I borrow the American Express card?"

"Why, dear?"

"Mom, don't be so nosy. I have needs."

"I should ask George. He wasn't too happy with that bill you and Pete ran up in Galveston."

"Whatever," said Kirstin, tonguing her gum to the opposite side. "That like wasn't our fault. We planned to stay for like the weekend and like ended up staying a week. Pete like went crazy over the bridal suite."

"I'm not criticizing, hon, I'm just saying that your father reminded me of the wolf at the door."

"Do I get the card or not?"

"Yes, but with a small string attached."

Kirstin emitted an exasperated sigh. "You're not going to like make me watch some boring movie."

"No, dear. The movie rule is for Scott, and I think it's working."

"I think you're like blind as toast."

Joyce giggled. "Blind as toast. I'll remember that one. I have such clever children."

"Mom, what is the bullshit price for the gold card?"

"I want you to talk to our next door neighbor. Don't scowl at me—it wasn't my idea."

"I didn't know we had a next door neighbor."

"Her name is Fran. She rents the cottage."

"Why would I talk to her?"

"Why, to get the card, dear."

"That's it? I go talk to her and I get the card?"

"Now dear, don't get huffy. Your father spoke with her and he thought it might do you good. She's a parent and your father thinks she has good judgment even if she comes on a bit strong."

"What would we talk about?"

"Well, I'm not sure, but I have a hunch you're pregnant again."

"So? I'll handle it. Mom, just give me the card."

"I can't dear. Your father took it. You'll have to see him. I'm sorry."

"Liar. You told me you had it."

Pete entered holding a beer. Without speaking to or nodding at Joyce he said, "Babe, we gotta go. You got the card?"

Kirstin stood. "I've been like wasting time talking to her and she doesn't have it. My dad is like making me jump through some hoop or something. Fuck."

Chapter 6

Kirstin, a Babe, Meets Fran, an Adult

Kirstin came to see Fran on a Tuesday evening. The house was quiet, the doors to the bedrooms off the hall closed.

"Like, where are your kids?" Kirstin asked.

"Studying," Fran said. "Come sit down."

"Okay," Kirstin said, "but like I have no idea why I'm here. My parents like told me to come over. My dad's been acting like weird since his heart attack, and my mom's like always weird."

Fran studied her radiant brunette hair, her pretty oval face, her curvaceous body, her endless legs, her full lips that, while pouting now, had the same endless potential as her legs.

"Tell me about yourself," Fran said.

"There's like nothing to say."

"Sure there is. You're what, twenty-two?"

"Twenty-one."

"Something must have happened in the last twenty-one years. Would you like some lemonade?"

"Do you have like a beer? I'm like nervous."

"Don't be, and no, I don't have any beer." Fran brought lemonade. "You were about to tell me something about yourself."

Kirstin uttered three or four more or less complete sentences about manicure, her apartment, and Pete, a tattoo artist, then crossed her legs to stare at Fran as if to say, "See, I've done what my father insisted I do and I've responded to your biographical probe and I haven't broken a sweat." She wondered if she had now been there long enough to justify leaving. She should sip some lemonade, then leave, she told herself.

"Yes," Fran replied, "your father told me all that. I was hoping for something more interesting; some view or opinion you hold, for example."

"About what?"

"About anything."

"What difference does it make?"
"Maybe none. It depends on the view."
"Why do you care?"
"It's a hobby of mine."
"Whatever," Kirstin said with undisguised impatience. She began staring intently into Fran's eyes, as this particular intimidation had proved so successful with her mother. Fran stared back.

"I didn't like high school," Kirstin said. "The boys were like immature jerks and the girls weren't friendly."

"High school boys can leave a lot to be desired," Fran agreed. "Why do you think the girls didn't warm up to you?"

"Because they were like dorky and dumb."

"And jealous?"

"Of what?"

"You're very attractive. Surely you know that."

"Yeah, the guys said that."

"And the girls may not have said it but they noticed. Believe me. Girls at that age have trouble with self image. I know because I was one. The pretty girls in our class didn't realize how inadequate I felt around them. So tell me about Pete."

"Total coolness," Kirstin said, sipping her lemonade. "What he like does with tattoos is amazing. He designed this like colorful alligator just for me. I'm like trying to decide where to put it. My folks can't stand him."

"Is that a plus for Pete?"

"There's also the Harley. It rocks."

An impression grew in Kirstin that Fran genuinely wished to know more, so she told her. Kirstin gestured a lot, used the word "like" about as often as she used the article "the," and talked non-stop for an hour and a half, ending with her current pregnancy. "I like cannot believe I'm telling you all this," she said. "My dad like said you might help, as if I need like help, but he says lots of bullshit things."

"I'll make you a deal," Fran said. "I have a five-year old daughter. If you'll agree to come here to baby sit her once in a while, I'll see what I can do to help. I'll pay you, of course, but there is one condition. Sometime while you're here, I'm going to confront

19

you. I'm going to ask you to sit where you're sitting, to not move for thirty minutes, and to not say one word. Is that a condition you can live with?"

"Like, I guess. What are you going to say?"

"I don't know."

"Like, what's your daughter's name?"

"Sarah."

"Where's the TV?"

"We don't have one."

"This is, like, weird," Kirstin said.

Chapter 7

Fran Lowers the Boom as Kirstin Neglects to Duck

In the ensuing days, Kirstin baby-sat six times, always at Fran's. James, age sixteen, hovered within hearing distance, though often out of sight. On each occasion Fran would leave for no more than an hour, sometimes to exercise and sometimes to grocery shop. Once home, she would go to her room and close the door, leaving Kirstin and Sarah to entertain themselves. Physically, Sarah favored Fran, with the same upturned eyes that would later, when she matured, influence her entire face. Kirstin played "manicure," which Sarah greatly enjoyed, and Sarah read out loud, which Kirstin appeared to enjoy less. At the end of each engagement, Fran paid Kirstin, who waited apprehensively for Fran to turn. On the morning Kirstin arrived to find Fran seated and Sarah out, she knew her time had come. Fran motioned her toward the chair.

"I've done some checking on you," Fran said. "You're quite bright."

"But school is like — "

Fran held up her hand, palm out. "Remember? You listen, I talk."

Kirstin nodded, sitting tensely across a small open space, as she might have waited for her name to be called at the dentist's.

"You need counseling, Kirstin. Lots of it over a long period of time. If and when you get it, your therapist is going to get you to talk about your childhood, your parents, your life, your interests, and after many months, possibly years, and untold amounts of money from your father and your insurance company, you may come to realize for yourself some of the things I'm going to tell you now. It's always better to reach your own conclusions than to have someone tell you what to think."

Fran paused, measuring Kirstin's attention level. "However, I am not a therapist, and I do not have months to devote to you or your problems. I have only this morning." She spoke casually, her

21

voice neither heavy nor upbeat. She might have been relating a recipe. "You are a bright girl, very attractive, which makes it even sadder that you will be one of life's losers. This is partly your fault, and partly the fault of your parents, who are both losers. Your father devotes his life to death and consumption. Because he lives well and employs others, it is not obvious that he is a loser, and you may have grown up thinking otherwise, but he is a loser, as you will eventually come to realize, but by then it will probably be too late. From what I know, your mother is a complete ditz. That's why you're speaking with me and not with her. Your parents are one thing you can't control. They are what they are, and none of us selects them. However, you are a product of a loser and a ditz, and that is not a combination likely to produce success.

"You are wasting the considerable number of assets you have. You're bright, as I said, which makes me wonder why you're using that very pretty mouth of yours primarily to gratify men who care nothing about you. You seem to have a very serious and persistent itch between your legs, and the number of men who have scratched it would probably shock me. All of this relates to what is called 'low self esteem,' but the way you are conducting your life will lead to lower self esteem until you finally crash or crack up. My hope is that you sterilize yourself so that you will not inflict this pattern on others.

"You have a serious speech impediment. Suppose I said the word 'catnip' in every sentence I uttered. I would sound idiotic, which is how you sound to me when you use the word 'like' as an adjective, an adverb, or an article. You may not know what those parts of speech are because I doubt they are discussed on MTV, but surely you are aware that you use the word 'like' excessively. That is also an insecurity, but one that is coupled with your indifference or inattention to how you are perceived by people other than men in heat. For someone with your intelligence to be studying manicure is an embarrassment. For someone with your advantages to be felt up, fucked and forgotten is an outrage, and it outrages me that you are not outraged. For you to bring your fetus to full term should be illegal, because my children and I need protection from the neglected child you will deliver.

"I've watched you with Sarah. You are gentle by nature, which is important. If you were now in your forties, as I am, I would predict that your situation is hopeless, but you're still young enough to turn yourself around. If I were you, which I am not, I would move back home, tolerate your parents, enroll in school, terminate this absurd pregnancy, and begin reading serious books. I doubt you will do these things, but they are what I would do."

Kirstin cried for some time as Fran looked on. Both remained seated, eight feet apart.

Chapter 8

Fran Loses Jim

Fran worked for the Centerfield *Sentinel*, a weekly newspaper with a circulation of 41,000. Her late husband, Jim, had been fatally injured in a two car accident a few weeks before Sarah's birth. Fran and Jim had been an item since high school in Piqua, Ohio, where Fran had been homecoming queen and Jim, a year older, had worked after school to help support his widowed mother. Theirs was the kind of incandescent romance that first loves produce, when everything is new and fresh and every nerve ending seems to be awakening to rapturous stimulation.

By Jim's senior year, they had discussed marriage, usually in the back seat of a car when the widows fogged. Jim had the grades for college but not the resources. He took a job in the local paper mill at union wages, bought a used car, and waited for Fran to finish school. Fran was certain her destiny was with Jim. When he held her, a peace settled over her that suggested forever, a feeling she could never explain to him or even to herself. In her senior year, when she realized she was pregnant, she waited for the peace she felt to be replaced by panic, but it never came. Something primal within Jim, or within her when she was with him, reassured her, even as they decided in tear-racked discussions lasting for days that they were not ready to be parents.

Fran stayed with her parents for two years after high school, commuting to a local college and spending what free time she had with Jim, who had been promoted twice at the mill. On the evening of his second promotion, he asked Fran to marry him. Their wedding was modest, attended mostly by friends from high school who still lived in Piqua, plus a few relatives they hardly knew. When Jim kissed his bride at the altar, Fran reached for the peace she found in his arms, and there it was. Jim's mother, by then seriously ill from a stroke, lived to see her only son married, but not much longer. With her death, Jim felt for the first time a freedom to

24

raise his eyes beyond the horizon of Piqua, the only placed he had lived or known. Fran suggested long-haul trucking as a way to see the country and, if they managed it right, a way to improve their income.

He financed a rig with sleeping quarters they named Cannibal, and for two years they drove together across the country, saving everything they earned that didn't have to go to keeping Cannibal on the road. On their last haul, they broke down in Twig. In the several days required for parts to be delivered, they drove around town long enough to like it. The money they saved would go a lot farther here, and Fran had been waiting for the right time to tell Jim they were expecting. They bought a starter home, put Cannibal back on the road with Jim five days a week, and made a life in Twig. Chip was born, then James, and to their mutual surprise, Sarah.

After the accident, Jim lingered in a coma for six months, during which Fran delivered Sarah, prepared the boys, and waited for the benediction. Jim's hospital bill exceeded $1.5 million dollars, a sum only partly covered by his insurance. Fran hired a lawyer, who secured the maximum amount available to her, $50,000, from one Ricky Tate, the construction worker who caused the accident. Tate lacked insurance. He had blown a .18 blood alcohol level in the patrol car that came to investigate. His record revealed three prior DUIs. Upon the advice of his lawyer, he expressed remorse to Fran and her children at his sentencing, three years in prison with two years suspended.

The *Sentinel* had granted Fran an extended leave of absence. She remained at home for eighteen months. When she returned, she worked three mornings a week, leaving Sarah with a neighbor who had baby-sat the boys when they were younger. She convinced the paper to let her work from home to fulfill her full time commitment, which she needed to support herself. The *Sentinel's* support did not extend to health insurance, however, and Jim's bills were followed by several mishaps with her active boys, the most serious of which occurred when Chip's bicycle was struck by a car, knocking him to the pavement and fracturing his hip. To repair the damage and to ward off a permanent limp, doctors had performed two extensive and wildly expensive surgeries. She sold

25

the house to pay the hospitals and doctors, to bank a reserve for emergencies, and to purge her life of the incessant reminders of Jim, whom she loved. She looked at six rental houses before selecting the one next to George and Joyce.

Chapter 9

Are You Busy Tuesday Afternoon?

One week after the lecture to Kirstin, Fran's doorbell rang. Kirstin stood outside. Her shoulders appeared a bit more squared than Fran remembered, but her eyes were softer. Fran asked her in, smiled as Kirstin greeted Sarah, and made tea.

"I'm trying," said Kirstin, studying the floor and gripping her wrist as though taking her own pulse. "I've been thinking about what you said, and I'm like really trying."

"Good," Fran said.

"But I have a problem. My mother sent Father Richards to see me. She told him I was like pregnant. He wants to pray for me, which is like okay, but he wants me to meet with this group of people about . . . you know . . . "

"When?"

"Next Tuesday afternoon. I think I'm doing the right thing, and I know you like agree, so I really don't want to meet with anybody."

"What does your mother say?"

"She says life is full of tough problems."

"Is that it?"

"She mentioned *Agnes of God*. And she thinks Father Richards is kinda cute."

Fran was grateful for Kirstin's riveted stare at the floor because the roll of her eyes was as pronounced as it was involuntary. "How can I help?" Fran asked.

"Do you think I should like go?"

"Yes."

"Why?"

"Because they will raise some issues you need to think about if you haven't already."

"It's not like it's my first abortion or something."

"All the more reason to think about it."

27

"Will you go with me?"

"If you like."

"Cool."

"On one condition. It's true that I gave you my view, but mine is not the only view. You must promise you will seriously consider what Father Richards and the others tell you."

"I can live with that."

"Then I guess it's a date. Tuesday afternoon. Keep trying."

Chapter 10

Meanwhile, in another hemisphere on the same planet

Abraham Rubiwitz was honorably discharged from the Israeli army just days prior to the outbreak of the Six-Day War in 1967. Immediately recalled for the conflict, he retired again when it ended. So swiftly did hostilities cease that he did not have a chance to cycle through his complete wardrobe of uniforms. He saw opportunity in the newly annexed West Bank, so he left Tel Aviv, the land of his birth, and moved to Nablus. There, he married, set up West Bank Properties, and settled in to raise a family. Over the next two decades, he was modestly successful financially, paying his bills and sending his two children to school. But when his wife suddenly left him, and the children left home, as children will do, his daily fate was to return to a house profoundly still. The silence threatened his sanity. His sole outlet was the business he had dabbled in, with varying measures of enthusiasm, for twenty years. Given a choice he perceived as either getting serious or becoming a middle age fool, he rededicated himself with single-mindedness that drove him to the very top echelon of Israeli real estate.

But lately, business was bad and very difficult. The open houses he liked to hold became a particular problem. As he had always done, he set out brochures, arranged a tempting assortment of cookies, and stood just inside the front door to greet prospective buyers. But increasingly, Palestinians showed up, and their interest in the listed property discouraged Jewish buyers from aggressively seeking to purchase. Conversely, because of ancient hostilities, the Palestinians were not happy to be shown kitchens, baths and bedrooms in the company of Jews. Words might be exchanged (Palestinian: "I'd get rid of these curtains"; Jew: "These curtains I love") and the dispute would carry over to the cookie display (Palestinian: "Oatmeal is the best"; Jew: "You can't beat a raisin cookie"). More often than not, tempers flared, leading someone to toss a cookie carelessly on the table in the general direction of

29

another, and before Abe (everyone called him Abe) could intervene, a full scale food fight broke out. Crumbs everywhere.

The complexities of showing the house paled beside those of actually selling it. On the rare occasions Abe managed to broker a deal, and a Palestinian buyer located a lender, such as the Seventh National Bank of Beirut, the Israelis invariably bombed the home before closing on the preemptive theory that it would sooner or later be used as a terrorist enclave. Naturally, the Palestinian buyer was reluctant to close after the home was destroyed, so the most Abe could do was retain the deposit, to which he was clearly entitled by virtue of the "bomb" clause in his standard contract. Jewish buyers were extremely rare, mainly because the price of the home was only the beginning of the expense and did not include such amenities as a 12 foot electrified privacy fence, guard dogs imported from Germany, surveillance cameras around the perimeter, nor the mining of the yard and the very expensive lessons to teach the children and the guard dogs the location of the mines. Abe was beginning to despair of ever achieving his dream, which was to make enough money to retire in Boca Raton.

Just as his angst reached its apex, Abe received a call that changed his life. Mordecai Samuelson identified himself as a representative of the Openly Yearning Explorers Vowing to Expatriate Yiddish (OYEVEY). Samuelson gave Abe a brief overview of his organization and requested a meeting. "How about the Shalom Café? You know it? Great lamb chops there."

"Wasn't it blown to smithereens a few weeks ago? That crazy woman?"

"It's under new management. They won't hit the same place twice. Like lightning."

Three days later, over lamb chops done medium rare with a precocious mint jelly on the side, Mordecai laid down some rules of engagement. "What I am about to tell you," he said, "cannot be repeated. Swear on your sainted mother's grave that you won't breathe a word of what you're about to hear."

"Actually, Mother's still alive."

"You're quibbling."

"Well, I just thought . . . ."

"Swear anyway. One day soon she will be dead, she'll be buried, yes? Make a down payment on her memory."

"This must be serious," Abe said, looking furtively around and thinking less about eavesdroppers than about Arabs wearing exploding vests.

"There's a matter of a commission," Mordecai said. "A big commission."

"You have my word," Abe responded, a little too quickly.

Despite the fact that they had the dining room to themselves, Mordecai motioned for Abe to lean forward. Heads together, Mordecai talked and Abe listened. Abe learned that OYEVEY's membership was composed of those who had come to believe that *peace would never become a reality* in the Middle East, that they, their children, and their children's children would continue to experience the *prolonged anxiety* of never knowing if they would get through a meal at a restaurant without being blown up by a suicide bomber before dessert was served, and that the time had come to do the right, the noble, and the very practical thing: relocate Israel to a safer place, specifically the United States.

"Let's be honest," Mordecai said, "the great experiment has not turned out so good. We can't sleep, we can't work, we can't even worship everywhere we want because of the violence. It's no way to live, I tell you."

"But what about Moses and the land of Zion?" Abe asked.

"Zion, Schmian," said Mordecai. "Moses didn't have to put up with these nuts in the West Bank. In his day, a plague here, some locusts there, yes, there were problems but not every minute of every day like we have now. Life is too short, my friend."

"But how can I help?" Abe asked. "I'm just a poor schmuck on commission."

"Yes, but you know real estate. We need someone who knows real estate. We need someone to go to the United States and find a suitable location to relocate the country. Are you interested?"

"Well, I could use such a commission, I won't lie."

"You've been to the United States?"

"Never."

"No problem. I'll get you maps. When can you leave?"

31

"Not until the end of the month. I have a closing set. Of course, it will probably be canceled once the house is destroyed, but I can't be sure until the explosion."

"I understand. If I could arrange to move up the date on which the house will be demolished, would that help?"

"Yes," said Abe, "then my calendar would be clear."

"Let me see what I can do. So, you're interested?"

"We need to work out the commission."

Mordecai waved his hand dismissively. "You worry too much. In a deal of this size, you'll make a king's fortune. Trust me."

But Abe wasn't certain, so he did extensive research on OYEVEY. He learned of a little-reported detail concerning the ceremony that took place in Tel Aviv at an art museum in 1948. When David Ben-Gurion, leader of the Zionist movement, formally proclaimed to his followers that the State of Israel had been born, all stood and applauded wildly save one: Moshe Stein. He sat glumly on his hands, wagging his head from side to side and muttering, "It'll never work. They hate us. They live in our back yards, our front yards, upstairs, downstairs; it'll never work. We need Plan B." Even less noticed at this summit was the presence of a moderate Palestinian delegation, also in favor of the State of Israel's birth. True, there were only four in the delegation out of 2.5 million Palestinians, but they were very influential. Three stood to applaud, while the fourth, Nosir Ararat, sat on his hands and muttered, "It'll never work. They hate us, they'll be living next door, and we'll have to pay retail for everything we buy from them. We need Plan B." While Abe was unable to trace Nosir's efforts, he soon learned that Moshe's Plan B was the establishment of OYEVEY, a long-term alternative to the chaos he predicted would ensue.

Moshe, a secular Jew, was not unmindful of the sacred ground at Jerusalem, the Wailing Wall, the Mount of Olives, the Sea of Gefilte, the Garden of Complaints, and the other treasured landmarks of the long-promised land, but for him these were less essential than some lower profile benefits, like living through the weekend and riding a bus that didn't stop prematurely due to a self-detonating passenger. From 1948 forward, he tithed 10% to OYEVEY, so that with compounding interest and an inflation factor that threatened the currency, that organization now boasted, fifty years later, a war chest in excess of 65 million shekels, or $961 dollars U.S. at current exchange rates. He was savvy enough to realize that buying New Israel in the United States would be difficult with these resources, but then he thought of Jesus, feeding the multitude with a couple of trout and some bread and he was much encouraged until he remembered that this was a Gentile myth foreign to his faith, not that he had much faith or that he believed the Jewish myths any more than those invented by goyim. "I'm going to need major cash," he concluded.

Major cash came, but as always with a price. Moshe was forced to turn over effective control of the organization and to accept the largely ceremonial, highly sinecurist post of Ex-Officio Senior Visionary, stripped of his parking space. The new players in OYEVEY brought a sense of urgency that Moshe lacked. They viewed the coming peace talks with the Palestinians as the kick-off, the face-off, the jump ball to the Apocalypse, and they sought liquid funds with the fervor of CEOs intent on beating the Street. They redefined aggressive, as everyone knew when they took 86% of the corpus of the trust established by Moshe and bought Power Ball lottery tickets in the U.S. They hit, sending the prospects for New Israel ("New I," as it was being called) soaring. Flush with cash, OYEVEY perceived its moment had arrived and delegated Mordecai with the task of finding a realtor.

As promised, Mordecai brought maps. He and Abe scanned them over lunch. It didn't take Abe long to convince his patron that when it came to real estate outside Israel, Abe was uniquely and spectacularly clueless. They ruled out Montana and Utah, both with plentiful land but too rocky, even for people who currently inhabited an uninhabitable desert. Alaska? "Let's put it this way," Mordecai said. "The sun doesn't set for four months, but at least the temperature climbs into the lower teens. How's that sound?"

They considered Ohio for its central location, but in that the amount of land needed required the better part of a densely populated state, they moved on. They studied California, and while they knew they could not afford land along the coast, eastern sectors of the state might be suitable. Texas? Mordecai urged Abe to give special attention to Texas, which looked like it had so much

33

undeveloped land that no one would even miss the 6000 square miles required.

"Well," said Mordecai when they had finished their research, "it looks like California or Texas. What do you think?"

"I'll begin packing," Abe said. "And thank you for the quick work on that house I had under contract."

Chapter 11

The Art of the Deal

Abe arrived at LAX and spent the better part of his first month in the US getting to know the Jewish community in and around L.A. They seemed friendly enough, but Abe soon came to realize that few held his organization in high regard. Most were Zionist to the core, strongly committed to the State of Israel in its current location, although a similar percentage seemed equally committed to staying in California where, with the exception of the occasional freeway pile-up in dense fog and houses perched atop the San Andreas Fault, life appeared relatively secure. Many considered Abe's mission impossible. As one southern California developer told him, "It takes an average of thirty four months to get approval for a carport here. Lots of luck on getting approval for an entire country."

Abe soon learned the truth of this statement. In his rental car, he drove the length and breadth of California. Wherever he found large tracts for sale, he met with county officials to ascertain the requirements for development. Soon, his mind reeled with the number of studies, plans, and hearings that would be needed. The times estimated for final approval ran from a conservative seventy-five years to a more realistic "never." He reported to Mordecai by phone that peace with the Palestinians would be quicker.

"Go to Texas," Mordecai urged. "From what I hear, they have no laws at all there."

Abe arrived at the Dallas-Fort Worth Metroplex on a Friday. In Dallas, he had something he lacked in California: a dues paying, card carrying, totally devoted member of OYEVEY who had, until three years before, lived in Jerusalem. This contact, Herb Golden, welcomed Abe to Texas.

"I believe in your work," Herb told Abe in the comfort of Herb's living room. The house was a sprawling rancher, ideally located in the Jewish block of Dallas. "I'd help you look myself, but

35

the truth is I don't know Texas so good and I'm needed at the store." Herb owned a chain of discount shoe outlets and was obviously doing quite well."

"Where to begin?" Abe asked.

"Ah," said Herb, "a very important question. Let me tell you one thing about Texans. They don't do so much business with strangers. You have to become one of them. Not really, of course, but you have to fit in so you don't look like a big, sore putz."

"What do you suggest?" Abe wanted to know.

Herb shrugged. "Change your name, change your clothes, learn a few local phrases; things like that. Study the Dallas Cowboys."

"Which is?"

"A football team. You've heard of them. They have the cheerleaders with the big kaboombas."

Abe nodded. "Doesn't sound too hard."

Herb and his wife, Sonya, insisted that Abe stay in their guest room as long as he wanted. On Monday, at Herb's suggestion, Abe went to meet with Ben Carter, a Dallas realtor.

"You will pardon the cliche," said Abe, "but you look Jewish."

"Indeed I am," said Carter. "I was Levi Epstein until I came here. You must change your name, especially if you're going to be negotiating with ranchers to buy their property. My good friend Herb is right. You need to blend in here."

So Abe became Art. Art Adams. He got a driver's license in his new name, then went shopping for clothes. He bought jeans, several very durable denim shirts with rhinestone buttons, a string tie, a steer skull clasp to hold the string tie in place, and a large Stetson with a rakish eagle's feather in the band. By the time he was fitted for lizard boots by a business associate of Herb's, he felt like a born-again Texan.

"How do I look?" Abe/Art demanded of Levi/Ben.

"Kosher, like you were born in Abilene."

"What's Abilene?"

"A town, but now that you mention it, we're going to have to do some work on your accent. Say bullshit."

"Bullshit."

"Yeah, that needs work. They judge a man here by how he says bullshit. It needs to be two words. Bull, but rhymes with yule, and drawn out. And shit, but more like sheet, like something you'd put on a bed. Buuule sheeeet"

"Bullshit."

"Keep working. It'll come."

The following week Art was ready to hit the road. From land records he had identified a 50,000 acre ranch outside Houston that was currently for sale. He drove from Dallas, and with each mile the countryside looked more austere than what was in his rear view mirror. He couldn't imagine anyone living there, nor charging real money to purchase the land. Flat, dusty, dry as bone. In other words, it reminded him very much of home. At 80 miles per hour, he blew by a sign that read "Centerfield."

An hour later, he drove up the long lane leading to the seller's house. A rancher met him at the door.

"How do. Name's Mac Travis. Come sit a spell."

"Buule sheet," said Art.

"Beg pardon?"

"Long drive," said Art, reconsidering.

"Yep. You had that hat long?" Mac wanted to know.

"I reckon," said Art. That was another phrase Levi/Ben had taught him.

Mac led him to a screened porch and served ice tea. When they were settled, he said, "What do you need with 50,000 acres? Lot of land, you know."

Art agreed. The stated purpose of his interest was key to success. No one tract of land could be acquired that would be large enough to comprise New Israel. The possible exception was the King Ranch, which was not for sale. Accordingly, he had to accumulate contiguous parcels, the way Disney had done when it bought Orlando for Disney World. And, like Disney, he had to keep the true nature of his effort a secret, because leakage of his real intent would send prices soaring.

"I'll be straight with you," said Mac. "No oil out there. I've had it drilled seven ways from Tuesday and it ain't produced enough to oil tweezers. Cattle is about all it's good for, and you don't strike me as a cattle man."

"I plan to put in olive trees," Art said.

Mac raised both eyebrows at this. "Olive trees?"

"Yep," Art said. "World demand for martinis is up 40%, but I guess I shouldn't be telling you because you might change your mind."

"Your plan is safe with me," Mac said, rubbing his weathered jaw. "I don't plan to get into the olive business. Those trees take much water?"

"Some," said Art.

"That's good, 'cause some is all that's out there in a good year. C'mon, I'll show you the place."

They got into Mac's dusty pickup and began a tour of the ranch. A trail of dust followed them. An hour later, they talked price.

"I want $5000 an acre," Mac said.

"That's quite high," Art countered. "Two hundred fifty million."

"Got my retirement to think about."

"Is there debt?" Art asked.

"'Bout the same amount of debt as oil," Mac replied, grinning.

"If you don't mind my asking, how much did you pay for it?"

"Fifty million, but that was thirty years ago."

"Cash?"

Mac winked. "When I said there was no oil on this place, I didn't mean no oil in Texas, if you catch my drift."

"Was it a cattle ranch when you bought it?"

"To tell the truth, it wasn't much of nothin' when I bought it. Owned by the Porkrind Trust. Just sitting here. I guess somebody must have had a plan, or maybe they just bought it thinking there must be oil somewhere. You sure you want this much property?"

"I'm looking for more, actually," said Art. "My client is a major olive grower."

Mac shook his head. "Must be."

They drove and drove, Mac pointing out variations in his herd and talking about the maintenance the fences required and Art thinking about palm-lined boulevards leading to the new capitol building for the Knesset. Toward mid-afternoon, Art offered an option, agreeing to pay $1,000,000 for the right to buy the place anytime in the next year for $4000 an acre. Mac agreed, and on their return to Mac's ranch house they drew up a one page document they both signed. Art wrote out check #101 from his new account at Republic Bank and the deal was done.

"You said you could use more land," said Mac as Art prepared to leave. "You should see Rusty. He's got the ranch next door. 'Bout the same size as mine, and his wife's been sick. I hear he's thinking of selling."

"Buuule sheeet," said Art.

Chapter 12

Fran Brings her Own Gavel to the Meeting

Father Richards headed the Committee On Unborn Gestating Humans (COUGH), an organization supported financially by Catholics, Baptists, and Republicans. The room into which Kirstin and Fran were ushered contained several of each. Father Richards, lean, about six feet tall, clean shaven but with a perfect beard had he chosen to grow one, opened with this prayer:

> Holy Father in heaven, we pray for Your daughter Kirstin. We pray that You will be with her and with us in her hour of decision. We pray also for the child within her. We will call this child Child, and if it be Your will for Child to be safely delivered into this world, we pray for Child's future here on earth, for Child's ultimate husband or wife, for Child's eventual children, grandchildren and great-grandchildren. Let us keep them all in our thoughts and our prayers here today.

He crossed himself several times, then looked at Fran. "Joyce didn't mention another person, but if you are a friend of Kirstin's you are welcome."

Fran said, "She has done some baby-sitting for me. I've advised her to get an abortion."The air grew noticeably warmer with this disclosure. Several committee members squirmed. One, an older man with a string tie, coughed. Father Richards smiled wanly, the patient if tired smile of the righteous about to feed a multitude.

"I see," Father Richards said. "We obviously hope to persuade her otherwise, as the sanctity of human life is dear to us and to our Lord."

"To me also," Fran said.

"Not dear enough, perhaps, given your advice."

"Dearer than you can know," Fran said, thinking not of Kirstin but of Jim.

A very fat woman with a large cross suspended from the folds of her neck spoke next. "You're advisin' her to commit murder is what you're doin'." This woman's vocabulary appeared to lack the letter "g."

Father Richards held up a pontifical finger. "Now, now, let's avoid recriminations. We're here to offer Kirstin our love and support. Kirstin, we know from your mother that you are considering an abortion. We want to accomplish two things in this meeting. First, we want to be sure you understand the violence that would be inflicted on Child if you carried through with such an act, and secondly, we want to show you all the resources that are available to Child should you decide to give Child up for adoption. If I may ask, how pregnant are you?"

"Seven weeks."

The fat woman fumbled through her file for the seven weeks slides. For the next forty-five minutes, the Committee pressed upon Kirstin its agenda. The man in the string tie continued to cough, but except for this distraction and incessant "amens" muttered around the table, the presentation went smoothly. At its conclusion, Father Richards looked expectantly across the table.

"That's one view," Fran said. "Here's another." She addressed Kirstin. "You have done a foolish thing that has resulted in a growth inside your uterus. Let's call it 'Spot,' because it is truly the size of a pin-point stain. It was put there by a man you do not love and who does not love you. It is the result of a chemical reaction predictable with a high degree of certainty when sperm is exposed to an ovulated egg."

"She's lyin'," hissed the fat woman.

Fran took no notice. "If your reproductive organs are not damaged by the abortion, which is a possibility, you can reproduce this same biological result with the same man or a different man, in a laboratory or in your womb."

Now Father Richards coughed. "That is heresy. Life begins at conception."

41

"I respect your view. Mine is that life begins at birth," Fran countered evenly. "Actually, life begins later, because the idea that an infant can survive when born is, of course, not accurate. It needs nurture, and if an adult does not provide it no infant ever born can survive more than a day or two. Based upon Kirstin's present state of emotional development and maturity, Spot will suffer neglect from the moment he or she becomes Child. Nor is nurture likely to come from the impregnator, because whatever skills he possesses in tattoo artistry are not those necessary to raise a functional human being. So before we mourn the loss of Spot, Spot Junior, Spot III and later descendents, perhaps it would not be asking too much to consider whether any of us currently trying to cope in this world, and that includes Kirstin, needs another unwanted group of dysfunctionals. I vote 'no,' but her vote matters most."

Father Richards said, "But adoption--"

"Is a priceless resource for those who choose it," Fran said.

"We will pray for you, Sister . . ."

"Fran. Thank you." She shifted her gaze from Father Richards to the fat woman. "I cannot debate heresy with you. You believe, which is your right, and if you believe that divine inspiration is responsible for the union of this immature girl and her tattoo artist boyfriend of the month, then you are right to voice your views. I believe in chemistry."

"You're headin' to hell, sister," said the fat woman. A chorus of grumbled amens echoed behind her.

"I've been there," said Fran. "You get used to it."

Fran and Kirstin drove home in silence. Kirstin thought about how Fran seemed to know things and to be unafraid to say what she knew. Fran thought about the abortion she herself had had at age seventeen, the saddest day in her life before Jim died. When they reached Fran's door, Kirstin said, "I guess I need to be more careful."

Fran patted her hand. "You need to keep your knees together."

42

Chapter 13

A Blue-Eyed Soul Meets the Old Seoul

Fran's boss at the *Sentinel* was Ed Abernathy, the founder's son. Abernathy had thinning hair, sky-blue eyes, a perpetual tan, and the largest earlobes Fran had ever seen. His reputation at UT during his college years, all six of them, bordered on legend. On a dare he succeeded in getting himself barred from 100% of the sorority houses on campus, not by keeping their co-eds out all night on drunken missions of lechery, which he did with regularity, but by sleeping with the house mothers and then jilting them in favor of one of their Greek counterparts. Shortly after he finally accumulated enough quality points to graduate, and after his father committed to a generous UT endowment, his father died, at which point the *Sentinel* fell into Ed's lap.

Abernathy arrived late, left after lunch each day to play golf, and divorced his wife on the eve of their twentieth anniversary. He traveled to the golf course in a silver Porsche at high rates of speed, shot in the low 80s, stayed at the nineteenth hole for lengthening periods, then drove home at the speed limit so as not to attract notice. His confidence that he would eventually sleep with Fran approached certainty. He found her professionalism sexy, as he mentioned at the Christmas party, one hand on a Scotch and the other on Fran's shoulder. Fran felt equally sure that this would never happen, as she mentioned on the morning following the Christmas party.

"Well," said Ed, a hangover evident in his bloodshot eyes, "if you won't sleep with me the least you can do is join the editorial staff."

"I like classified ads," Fran said.

"And you do a great job with them."

"So why change?"

"We need help formulating . . . opinions."

Fran knew this to be true. The paper had a reputation for implacable stances on holidays, war heroes, Texas football (high school, college, and pro), and cooking contests, particularly barbeque. On issues such as taxes, public works, education, health care, urban sprawl, the environment and national defense, the *Sentinel* did little more than "putz around," as Ed himself admitted.

"It's so damn hard to know what to say," he lamented, tugging on an earlobe. "You have to study all those . . . issues."

In truth, Ed avoiding reading, the *Sentinel* or anything else. His grasp of the day's news came from CNN, which he watched faithfully so as not to be embarrassed on the golf course by ignorance of some major international development. On a map of the world he could not distinguish between Belgium and Botswana. His knowledge of history stopped at the border of his own life, which was to say Eisenhower's second term. He confused the Roosevelts because he thought San Juan Hill had been a battle fought in World War II. A member of his editorial staff had once asked what position the paper should take regarding the stationing of U.S. troops in Korea. "I'm against it," Ed said. "If we send them over, they'll stay over. Vietnam proved that." Upon being reminded that the U.S. had maintained 35,000 troops in Korea for going on half a century, he said, "I rest my case."

"If only CNN had editorials," he said to Fran on their fourth or fifth discussion about her future. "You seem to enjoy keeping up with things. We really need your help."

"Enough to provide health insurance?"

"No, not that much," Ed said.

Chapter 14

A Podiatrist in the Family?

Scott located a website dedicated to those with fetishes falling outside of mainstream fetishes, its major enhancement being a sophisticated and detailed search function. Within minutes Scott located "1sicksize9," who not only had a thing for women's orthopedic shoes, but startlingly did not confine that passion to black shoes. This expansion of the universe intrigued Scott because he had heretofore found stimulation in shoes of one color, and he wondered if 1sicksize9's liberality had social or psychological significance. He e-mailed 1sicksize9 at once. Soon after they began trading photographs, at which point Scott realized that his e-pal was a sophisticated and dedicated collector. As he downloaded, Scott gazed wide-eyed at page after page of knees, tibias, fibulas and shoes. He entered a state of frenzied arousal, the source of which he traced to the strangeness of 1sicksize9's collection. While virtually all Scott's prized photos featured women in bulky support hose, these new photographs featured orange, navy and green orthopedic shoes whose owners wore sheer hose and even no hose. The sight electrified him, whetting his appetite for all 1sicksize9 could supply. That turned out to be quite a bit, particularly when Scott disclosed that he was in a position to pay for choice shots. Not only was he coming to appreciate the sophistication of colored shoes, but he also discovered an emerging zest for the taper of the calf. On a rainy afternoon, while George worked and Joyce shopped, he downloaded what became his ultimate pin-up: a sleek, red corrective shoe (possibly addressing pigeon toe, he thought) with a slightly elevated heel, the ankle covered by a white Bobbi sock and the calf turned in such a way as to highlight an athletic musculature. "My god," he whispered, then went into the bathroom.

His fetish remained a secret until the day Remedios found the durable medical equipment catalog in his bathroom while

45

cleaning it. As she spoke no English, and Joyce spoke one phrase of Spanish—"bonus diez"—its significance was not immediately apparent. Nevertheless, Joyce had heard a discussion on Oprah that seemed to suggest that children's reading material often offered insight into their minds and personalities. Enlightened, she raised the subject at dinner one evening.

"It's a very strange thing to read, Scott. Pictures of wheelchairs and crutches and those adjustable beds that go up and down."

"Maybe I'm thinking about becoming a doctor," he said.

"Are you?" asked George.

"Maybe. They help people and stuff like that."

"They make a lot of money, those doctors do," offered the voice of Joyce.

"Medical school," said George. "That's expensive. I'll have to bury a lot of people to pay for that."

Scott spoke. "Centerfield Hospital has an intern program. I checked it out last week. I'm going to volunteer there a few days a month."

"That's wonderful," Joyce said, raising her wine glass in salute.

"Good idea," George agreed. "If Kirstin had that kind of get-up-and-go she wouldn't be in the fix she's in now. Where in the hospital will you be working?"

"The geriatrics unit."

"What's that?" Joyce asked.

"Geriatrics. Old people," Scott said.

Joyce folded her napkin. "Oh, Scott, I am soooo proud of you. Helping old people who are no longer as young as they used to be. Now that is awesome. I can't wait to tell your grandmother."

"She hasn't come to see us in a long time," Scott said.

"I didn't think you liked her," Joyce said.

"Oh, she's okay. I wouldn't mind her visiting. How are her feet?"

"Her feet?"

"Yeah. Just asking. That's a big problem at the hospital. Old ladies have problems with their feet. They need special shoes."

"Oh," said Joyce, "you mean those black clumpy things."

"The same," Scott said. "But they're not all black."

"They're not? How interesting," said Joyce. Then, dreamily, "Our Scott a doctor."

Chapter 15

A Father Says Uncle

Fran answered the phone.

Father Richards said, "I suppose you've heard."

"Heard what?"

"Kirstin went through with it. I hope you're happy."

"I'm sad, but it was the right decision for her."

Father Richards coughed. "Pardon me," he said.

"If you're calling me to pedal some guilt, Father, you're wasting your time. I learned that trick a long time ago."

"You're a very persuasive woman, Fran. I wish we had you on our team."

"Kirstin made her own decision, and for what it's worth she made it before she ever spoke with me."

"I wasn't referring to Kirstin. We had a resignation from COUGH right after you spoke. We lost a Republican."

"There are more of them out there."

"Yes, but few as wealthy as Todd Melville. He's been one of our major donors. In the world of non-profit funding, there are minnows and there are whales. Todd's a whale."

"I can't imagine that had anything to do with me."

"Evidently, it did. His letter of resignation said that he was quitting in view of the doubts you raised for him. He says he's rethinking his position. I'm meeting with him to talk him out of it, of course."

"Naturally. Father, I'm curious as to why you're telling me this."

"Because you have a powerful weapon of persuasion at your disposal. I pray that you use it wisely."

Chapter 16

Ed Catches Fire

Ed Abernathy stood silently in front of Fran's desk until she noticed him. "I know you want to stay in classifieds," he said, "but this is an emergency."

"I understand emergencies," she said. "And emergency rooms."

"You're not going to start on that health insurance business again, are you?"

"What's the problem?"

"The fire department. They're talking about converting the Centerfield Volunteers to a paid, professional unit." He pointed out the window, in the general direction of 'they'.

"Would that be good?"

"How should I know? That's the emergency. The *Sentinel* needs to be out front on this and someone has to look into it."

"Why me?"

"Did you read last week's editorial?"

"On vinegar-based barbeque sauces?"

"I rest my case. We can't screw around on this fire department issue. I want this newspaper on record as firmly and unequivocally for or against it, and I don't much care which. You simply must help us."

"Ed, have you considered the possibility that one day you may have a fire, and that this decision could affect whether it is extinguished?"

Ed paused. "No. Should I? I have a 1:30 tee time. Think it over."

Chapter 17

Channeling, in Tongues

Fran worked at home on the morning a large truck parked in George's and Joyce's driveway. Workmen from the Interstellar Communications Group installed a satellite dish on the roof, replacing the old one.hh

When Fran went running later that week, she spotted Joyce outside, speaking to Jose, the gardener. Joyce saw Fran.

"Hello," Joyce said. "Have you been running?"

"Yes," Fran said, flushed below her headband and just beginning her cool-down. "And you?"

"Yard work. We got a new satellite."

"I saw them put it in. Did the old one break?"

"Oh, no," Joyce said. "George ordered this one because it gets two hundred more channels."

"How many did the old one get?" Fran asked.

"I forget exactly. I think about four hundred."

"Isn't that a lot of channels?"

"Yeah. But the new dish shows things we just can't get here."

"Such as?"

"These soap operas from Thailand. They come on at 3 a.m. The people are so, I don't know, exotic or something."

"They're in Thai, I assume?"

"Thailand."

"No, I mean the language."

"I guess so. It isn't English."

"Doesn't that make it hard to understand?"

Joyce laughed. "Impossible, really. Except, you know what? I think their problems must be a lot like our problems, the way they look nervous when they know it's bad news and stuff."

Fran reached down, held her ankles, and as she stretched her hamstrings said, "I find TV a waste of time."

50

"Really? What do you do at night?"

"Read."

"I read a book at the beach this summer. They talked about it on the Today Show and it sounded good so I bought it."

"Was it good?"

"It was fabulous. I guessed the ending, because I have a real gut feeling for things like that. George says so himself. I told George, 'her brother killed him and put the body in the water tower' and bingo! Sure enough."

"That's a talent," Fran said.

"You can tell by the things they try to slip by you. Like the woman mentioning how the water tasted funny, but she only said it that one time and if you just read along and didn't pay attention to little details then you miss it. Did you hear that Kirstin is moving back?"

"When?"

"Next month."

"How do you feel about it?"

"One side of me is happy, of course. She's my daughter."

"And the other side?"

"Kirstin has been dealing with some tough problems. You know kids. It can be depressing, and George says we'll have to put off the house addition because of the wolf at the door."

Chapter 18

A Senior Moment for the Tooth Fairy

Kirstin came to see Fran a few days after moving back home. "How is it over there?" Fran asked. They sat in Fran's den, where the Fafalone residence was visible through a window.

"Like strange. It's a good thing the house is so big because they leave the TVs on all night. Lots of oriental women crying. I wanted to tell you I've been seeing a doctor. You know, like a shrink."

"That's a positive step," Fran said. "Male or female?"

"A woman."

"Good choice. You like her?"

"I guess. It's not such fun."

"No, and it won't be."

"She says I have lots of issues."

"Most of us do. Keep at it."

"How are things with you?" Kirstin asked.

Fran smiled. "Fine. Thank you for asking. My boss wants to promote me, but since it means more responsibility at the same pay I'm not buying champagne."

"What would you be doing?"

"Editorials."

"You don't like editorials?"

"Actually, I do. Sometimes. I'm not sure why I'm not more enthused."

"Maybe it's like you say, the money issue."

"Could be. Maybe I just resent the idea that he thinks he can get something for nothing. Walk with me to the laundry room. I need to toss some clothes in the dryer."

Kirstin stayed another twenty minutes, during which they spoke of Sarah's lost tooth and Fran's forgetting to put a quarter under her pillow and how she felt guilty all day because Chip, who was thirteen, had told Sarah it was proof that the tooth fairy didn't like her. When Kirstin left she squeezed Fran's hand and Fran squeezed back.

Chapter 19

Chip's Procrastination Leads to Confrontation on Aisle Six

"I can't do it," Fran announced to Ed.

"You've got to," Ed said. He sat at his desk looking for a pen.

"It's no good," she said. "At first I thought it was the pay, but I've thought it through. It's the fire department. I realized that the decision over the fire department is going to boil down to money, plain and simple. Can Centerfield afford to pay them or can we continue to rely on volunteers. It's the kind of decision accountants and city managers make. It lacks . . . sizzle. I'm a . . . moralist. I like issues that involve right and wrong."

"Great," said Ed, slamming his desk drawer. "Where are we going to find those?"

But within days of assuring Ed that moral issues abounded, even in Texas, Fran ran headlong into one. Chip, having put off a science project until the last possible minute, asked her to get him some needed supplies. She drove to Wall-More.

As she selected poster board and the indelible pens Chip needed, she overheard a woman a few feet away, in school supplies. The woman was young facially, perhaps late twenties, exceedingly large, and wore a dress with dimensions Fran associated more with sheets than clothes. She stood behind a shopping cart, her ham-sized hands resting on its push bar. A few feet from her, a small boy, perhaps six, fingered a box of crayons.

"Put 'em back, Jerome," yelled the woman. "I ain't telling you again." The boy gave no sign of hearing. "Jerome!" the woman yelled, more insistently. The boy continued to turn the box of crayons over in his hands. The woman stepped toward him. For a moment the boy disappeared from Fran's sight, hidden by the gargantuan haunches that propelled the woman forward. Suddenly, the woman raised an arm and brought her hand down solidly across the boy's head. The slap against his ear caused Fran to instinctively bring her hands to her head, as if by shielding her ears she could protect his.

"No," Fran called out, but not before the woman launched the other hand, catching the boy on the opposite ear and knocking him to the floor. Crayons skittered across the aisle. He began a loud, wailing cry of anguish. The woman turned.

"Are you crazy," screamed Fran, unaware of how loud her voice had grown. "He's a child."

The woman glared. "Kiss my ass, bitch," she said. "Mind your own goddamn business. When I say something, he better listen."

"I doubt he can hear you. He's probably deaf by now."

The woman drew nearer, then patted her purse. "Bitch, I'll cut you. I ain't taking none of yo' shit so outta my face." Store patrons watched from a distance, but no one approached.

Fran found herself shaking, her knees unsteady and her heart pulsing against her chest cavity. The woman now stood close enough to touch. Fran drew a deep breath. "That would be a big mistake," she said.

A scornful half-smile crossed the woman's face. "I said I'll cut you."

"That will only delay your seeing Jerome in the foster home."

"What you mean foster home? He lives with me."

"Not for long," Fran said, breathing easier. "I'm with Centerfield Social Services, Children's Division, and we deal with abused kids like Jerome. I just need your name and address so I'll know where to send them to pick Jerome up. I know just the foster family for a boy like him. And if you still want to cut me you can kiss him goodbye forever. Now, your name is . . .?"

The woman took a step back, then muttered, "I ain't giving you nuttin."

Fran said breezily, "Oh, it doesn't matter. I'm sure the store people know who you are."

The woman turned. She approached Jerome, held out a massive hand, the first assault weapon, and helped him from the floor. She lumbered for the door, Jerome in tow, without packages and without looking back.

55

Fran checked with the night manager, who could not identify the woman by name but confirmed she shopped there often. Fran, sitting in her car in the parking lot, locked her door and wondered how much trouble she could be in for impersonating a public official. Did Centerfield even have a Social Services Department?

Chapter 20

There's a Lot of it Going Around

Father Richards invited Todd Melville for coffee. Melville had the trim fitness of a distance runner, a smooth, baby-faced jaw that jutted forward even as his pale green eyes receded. They met at Starbucks, newly opened in Centerfield and yet another sign of the town's maturity.

"How about those Astros?" Father Richards began. He didn't follow sports, but had come to think of this as an ice breaker.

Melville eyed him skeptically. "Four game losing streak. Nothing new there."

"No, no, same old 'Stros," Father Richards said, adding cream and sugar liberally to the cup in front of him. He coughed softly to clear his throat. "So, you're leaving the Committee. We hate to lose a good man, Todd."

"It's been coming for a while, Father. I think I'm having a crisis of faith. That woman, Fran, pushed me over the edge, but I've been leaning over it for some time. I'm just not sure of anything anymore. That's not good for a Republican."

"We all have such periods. It's important to work through them. I'd like to help if I can."

"Thanks," said Melville, who had turned a modest income from an oil lease into a multimillion dollar computer software corporation. "I've been so busy building my business that I haven't had much time to sort some things out. I plan to take that time now."

"Can't you do that as a member of COUGH?"

"I don't think so. The people there are pretty . . . committed, as they should be, I suppose. I just question whether things are as black and white as people like Agnes paint them." Agnes spoke without using the letter "g."

"Of course they are."

57

Todd Melville smiled, then sipped his coffee. "I'm thinking of forming my own group, dedicated to exploring all sides of these thornier issues. A social think tank, a Platonic society where cloudy things are held up to the light."

Father Richards made a guttural noise that sounded like a low growl. "How interesting," he said, excusing himself to hit the rest room. On his return, his foot struck a table leg, stubbing his toe. "Shit," he said under his breath. The day was proving a difficult one. Seated again, he asked Melville if he had recruited anyone into his planned organization.

"Not yet. I want to come up with a name first."

"Any candidates?"

"I'm considering the Society for New Ethical Enlightenment with Zen Emphasis."

Father Richards brought his cup down on the table hard. "But that spells SNEEZE," he said. "You're mocking COUGH."

Melville smiled again. "Partly, but hey, we're all a little sick anyway, don't you think?"

Chapter 21

Imelda Slept Here

Joyce stood at her dining room window watching Dwight LaCalle exit his Lexus and walk toward the front door, which she opened as he reached for the doorbell.

"We've been waiting for you," she exclaimed, a little breathless. Dwight was the Fafalones' architect, and Joyce had set her mind and heart on the addition, Kirstin or no Kirstin. "George," she called out, "Dwight's here."

"In the kitchen," said George, seemingly at some distance.

Dwight's attire staked his claim to a front row seat in the theater of modern architecture. He wore black slacks, a form-fitted white silk shirt with priest's collar buttoned at the neck, swept back, space age sunglasses and hair held rigidly in place with an alarming quantity of sculpting gel. He entered the foyer as if assuming command of a space ship. Invisible eyes swept across what might have been instrument panels, checking altitude, confirming trajectory, synchronizing orbit re-entry calculations, nodding at gauges showing adequate solid fuel booster reserves. "Nice," he said, leading Joyce through her house in the general direction of George's voice.

"Sit down," George said as they entered. "I'm just finishing up breakfast. Sweet roll?"

"No thanks," Dwight said. "It's nice to be back here. I had forgotten what a fabulous job I did on the last addition."

"Ten years ago," George said. "We like to keep it fresh."

"Yes, fresh," said the voice of Joyce. "Something daring is what I have in mind."

"Joyce, pass me that that cinnamon bun, will you? Like she says, something daring."

"What did you have in mind, specifically," Dwight asked.

Joyce sat down at Dwight's elbow, leaning forward. "George wants what he calls his Irish Pub room, and I want a sun

59

room with lots of sky lights. Then we want a guest room with baths and a separate access."

George spoke, still munching his cinnamon bun. "I thought we had a guest room."

Joyce laughed. "Just like a man," she said. "George, you know I used that room to set up all that exercise equipment you bought me for Christmas. We couldn't ask guests to stay in there."

"I thought you got rid of that stuff."

"Don't be silly. I wouldn't give away something you spent time selecting as a gift."

"So that stuff is still up there?"

"Of course. That's why we haven't had guests."

George said, "Let's be sensible about what we're asking Dwight here to do for us. If we can't use the guest room because of the exercise equipment, we don't just build another guest room. Let's build a workout room so we can use the guest room we already have. We'll put a sauna in it, and a wet bar. It'll be nice. We can do that, can't we Dwight?"

"Anything you like," Dwight said.

"You're right," said Joyce to George. "Oh, this is so exciting."

"I'd like to take a look at the . . . space," Dwight said. His reverence for the word "space" gave it a shrine-like dimension.

"You mean upstairs?" Joyce asked.

"Yes. Let's see it."

George grabbed the last cinnamon bun on their way out. "Addictive," he said to Dwight. "You gotta try one."

They walked upstairs with George in the lead. At the top of the stairs he turned left.

Joyce called to him, "George, that's not the way to the guest room."

George laughed as he caught his breath. Turning to Dwight, he said, "Oh, yeah. I don't come up here much, to tell you the truth. This is Joyce's turf." Dwight smiled.

Morning sun highlighted the texture of the carpet in the guest room, along with some dust on the treadmill, for which Joyce apologized, vowing in undertones to speak to Remedios about the importance of thorough dusting.

60

"A lovely room," Dwight said. "Any guest would feel right at home here."

Joyce beamed. "I'm glad you like it." She walked to the closet for no apparent reason and slid open the door. On the lower shelf she saw five pairs of black orthopedic shoes, neatly aligned. "Where did those come from?"

George and Dwight ventured over. "Beats me," George said. "They look like something your mother would wear."

"I don't think so," Joyce said. "Mother isn't fond of black."

"Some guest, maybe?" Dwight suggested.

Joyce shook her head. "No one has used this room in years."

"Let's see the rest of the . . . space," Dwight said. "We need to decide on where to locate the Irish Pub, the solarium, and the spa."

As Joyce slid the closet door shut, she said, "You don't suppose Kirstin put those there, do you George?"

"Beats me," he said. "Maybe you should ask her."

Chapter 22

*Fran Learns the Power of the Pen
and the Distance to New Mexico*

"Okay, Fran, this is getting serious," Ed Abernathy announced to Fran one morning. "Come into my office."

Fran had been into Abernathy's office only a handful of times, principally because Abernathy had been in it only slightly more often. He liked to work at the desk outside his office, which accommodated a secretary when he had one, as he currently and usually did not. Fran followed mechanically, sensing trouble.

When the door closed behind them, Ed said, "I didn't want the other employees to hear this. First thing you know they'll want health insurance too."

"Many of them do," Fran said.

"And I want them to have it, but we've got a very expensive problem on our hands here." He pulled on his earlobe for emphasis on the word "expensive."

"Which is?"

"As you know, Millie has breast cancer." Millie worked in layout.

"I know. She's doing better, though."

"Which delights me, but what you may not know is that we have three other employees at the moment with serious medical problems, and each of them has a family with some disease or another. The cost of insurance for a little old paper like the *Sentinel* would be astronomical. Believe me, because I've shopped it. But, since I can't afford it for everyone, I'm trying to take care of you, at least. I've arranged for you to join an HMO."

"Can you do that? I mean, if you offer it to me, don't you have to offer it to everyone?"

"How should I know? I'm not a lawyer. I'm just a businessman trying to get some editorials written."

"I wouldn't feel right with a benefit the others don't have."

62

"Don't be a sap. Some of the others are covered by their spouse's policy. Besides, you haven't heard the details of your plan yet. Let's call it experimental. If it works for you, we'll put everyone on it, I promise."

"When does my coverage begin?"

"As soon as you fill out the paperwork." He handed her a sheaf of paper from the briefcase on the credenza.

Back at her desk, Fran noticed first that her employer had been listed as the Mountain View RV Camp and Resort. After perusing the rest of the materials, she returned to Abernathy's office.

"Like I say, I'm not a lawyer," he said somewhat defensively. "The accountant says to do it this way, otherwise we have to cover everyone. From now on your paycheck will come from the Mountain View RV Camp and Resort."

"Which is where?"

"Outside of Albuquerque. I'm a partner in that deal. Trust me, this will work out."

"I'm looking over the list of enrolled physicians. I have to drive only 800 miles to see a family practice doctor."

"I'm sure they have people in this area. I'll check. In the meantime, can you *please* think up some position we can take. If not the fire department, some other issue. I'm taking heat at the golf course over this and I need to prove we're serious."

Fran surprised him. "Okay, I'll do it," she said.

"For this week's edition?"

"Count on it."

She returned to her desk, closed the door, and did not emerge until she had completed the following, which ran in the *Sentinel* verbatim.

A House Divided
When Abraham Lincoln said "A house divided against itself cannot stand," it is doubtful he had in mind the relationship between a muscular, abusive parent and a helpless child, but the metaphor holds.

She went on to describe the scene she had witnessed in Wall-More, ending with this:

> A nation that turns upon its children is in a death spiral. We need to seek out the Tanyas of our community and remove from their control those powerless victims of what is often mindless immaturity, but is sometimes evil itself. That will not be easy in Centerfield because we lack a child protection agency, and we need one.

"Well, kiss my cactus," Ed said. "I can't wait for the boys at the golf course to see this. It's just what we need, Fran. Hard hitting, no pun intended, and no mention of barbeque."

"I couldn't work it in," she said.

The *Sentinel* hit the supermarket racks on Thursday morning, and twenty-four hours later Fran had the first reactions to her piece. They came mostly from women, expressing surprise that Centerfield lacked something as essential as child protection and relating experiences similar to Fran's. Ed reported seeing the town manager at the fifteenth tee. "He promised to look into it. Get started on next week's editorial."

"Any progress on my HMO?" she asked.

"I learned they have approved specialists all over Houston."

"That's a lot closer than Albuquerque, at least."

"There's still a small hitch."

"How small?"

"Manageable, I'm sure."

"For you or for me," Fran wanted to know.

"For us. We're a team."

"And that would be . . .?"

"What they call the primary care physician has to be in Albuquerque, otherwise they will ask too many questions. But the good news is that they can refer you to some great doctors only an hour away."

"This isn't going to work," Fran said. "I might have to make it the subject of my next article."

Ed did not laugh.

Chapter 23

Fran Steps Out, Watches Step

In the years following Jim's death, Fran refused all date requests, not that there were many. As a middle-aged single mother of three living at the margin, she held few cards that made for a winning hand in the poker game known as Second Time Around. It did not help that she still loved Jim, a fact she spoke of only to her children. Then, quite unexpectedly, she received a phone call from Todd Melville.

"You don't know me, but we've met," he said. "I was a member of COUGH until recently. I was there on the day you came with Kirstin."

"I wish I could say I remember you clearly, Mr. Melville —"

"Please, call me Todd"

" — but that was a stressful day for everyone."

"Of course. I thought maybe we could go out for coffee."

"If you want to pick up where the COUGH meeting left off —"

"Not at all. Not a word about COUGH or its agenda, I promise. I just admired the way you handled yourself and spoke your mind. I decided that day I'd like to get to know you better. That's all."

"Coffee sounds fine."

They met at Starbucks, at a table not far from where Father Richards had endeavored to keep Melville as a member of the flock. Upon seeing him stand as she approached, Fran placed him, something she had not been able to do earlier. During Kirstin's inquisition he had been seated on Fran's left, near Agnes of the missing "g". She could not recall him having spoken, a recollection he confirmed as soon as they were seated and had ordered coffee.

"You brought it up," he reminded her with a smile.

65

"Yes, I did. Now we can move on."

"Tell me about yourself," he urged.

Fran found herself speaking about her work for the *Sentinel*, some recent books she liked and a couple she didn't, noticing as they talked that Melville was both attractive and attentive. He asked good questions and he followed her answers. My God! she thought, he's a conversationalist. She omitted any reference to her home, her family, or her late husband. My God, she's not a victim, he thought.

"And you?" she asked.

Melville spoke about his computer company, his rabid interest in sports, his love of Gulf fishing, and his favorite movies. At the end, he said, "I'm divorced. That was painful but I'm through it so I've moved on."

"Any kids?"

"No. That made it easier, for sure."

"How long ago?"

He looked up, into the circular fan above them. "Three years in April."

Aha, thought Fran. The ex-wife syndrome. Now I'll hear endless drivel about love gone wrong with a woman that will sound like she's crazy as a pretzel and I'll be left to wonder why he married her in the first place.

But he did not speak of his ex-wife. Fran had planned to stay an hour and stayed for almost two. When they parted they shook hands.

Chapter 24

Kirstin Gives Pete Road Directions

Kirstin's return to the Fafalone residence created certain adjustment problems for Scott, who in her absence had become accustomed to a complete run of the house with the exception of the kitchen, the den, and his parents' bedroom, all downstairs and the only three rooms in which George and Joyce spent any appreciable time. For one thing, he and his girlfriend, Allison, could no longer run nude up and down the upstairs hallway playing a game Scott wickedly called Thai Me Up, Thai Me Down in belittlement of the foreign soap operas Joyce watched on the enhanced satellite service. Now, whenever Allison stayed over and they carelessly left a door open, so that Kirstin heard the moans issuing from Scott's room, they were treated to a lecture from her on the risks of uncontrolled sexual frenzy. Scott responded by saying, "Whatever," and accused her of smoking bad marijuana. Kirstin assured them that she had given up the weed altogether and that she spoke with a credibility they should not ignore. During one such confrontation, Kirstin noticed that Allison was not completely nude in that she wore black, clumpy shoes, but Allison dismissed Kirstin's comment with a laugh while Scott remained silent.

Kirstin mentioned to Joyce that she was concerned about some of Scott's interests, but Joyce reassured her by pointing out that Scott had matured in that he no longer watched slasher movies with his former frequency. "He's grown up so much," Joyce said, mentioning once again the hospital volunteer work that had led Scott into "the field of medicine."

"Mother, he's a pervert."

Joyce laughed. "When you get to be my age, with children of your own, you'll get used to these phases kids go through. It's very normal. If you don't believe me, you should watch *The Big Chill*."

67

Scott regretted Kirstin's glimpse into his fetish. He worried that seeing Allison in orthopedic shoes would lead to further prying, so he took greater precautions to hide his collection. He resolved to keep them in the guest room closet, where he had stored some of his original purchases. He also became more guarded in his internet usage, reminding himself to sign off more often and to change his password. His communications with 1sicksize9 continued to flourish, to a point that he began to entertain the notion of meeting him. Scott certainly did not need Kirstin's input on this prospect, as she seemed to him to be turning into "some flaky do-gooder."

Kirstin's return also created adjustment problems for her. Severing her relationship with Pete, the tattoo artist, had not gone smoothly. Pete insisted he had "feelings" for her and grew irate when she asked him not to call or visit. He came anyway, his arrival announced by the un-muffled engine roar from his chopped Harley. His usual attire consisted of jeans and a skimpy vest of sorts that allowed him to display some neck ware and the leopard tattooed on his chest. This leopard, multicolored and fierce in the artistic tradition of velvet Elvis, had once been a source of stimulation for Kirstin. Now it served as a source of disgust. The more Pete guided the conversation to his plan to have Xanadu tattooed on his back, the less Kirstin tolerated him. "Did I actually like this bozo?" she asked herself. Then she put the same question to Pete. He pondered it.

"Hey, Kirst, we had some good times."

"You had some good times. I had some wasted months and an abortion. And don't call me Kirst."

"Come on, Kirst, what's eating you? You used to like it when the leopard did the mambo, remember?"

"Don't remind me. Pete, you need to leave. It's over, and it's time for you to like move on."

Somewhere along the highway Pete traveled he had acquired the politicians' habit of referring to himself in the third person. "Oh, no. Pete don't give up on something that catches his eye. Just because you're sitting here in your daddy's expensive house and you've walked out on your old friends don't give you the right to flip Pete off like he was trash."

Kirstin rolled her eyes, at which Pete grabbed her wrist hard, squeezing and twisting. She winced, at first alarmed and then strangely comforted by the pain. Fran had predicted that getting her life straight would inflict some torture, and here was more. Bring it on, she thought.

Chapter 25

Ed Warns Fran to be Careful Where
She Points a Loaded Cursor

Fran discovered she liked writing editorials. To her
surprise, she looked forward to Thursday, when she drove to the
supermarket to purchase the *Sentinel* to read the piece to which she
had applied the finishing flourishes only twenty-four hours earlier.
She wished she could overhear the comments of those who read it,
and in this she acquired a voyeur's interest in her readership. She
knew many, indeed most, never read the editorials at all, and
purchased the paper solely for the coupons, the obituaries, or local
gossip not reported by the Houston *Chronicle*. But the movers and
shakers in Centerfield, whoever they were, did read them,
notwithstanding the fact that they neither moved much nor shook
anything. In all probability, they were the same people who played
golf with Ed Abernathy. The fact that a foursome of businessmen
would occasionally linger over a putt to comment on some thought,
opinion or insight moving straight from her mind and heart onto
the printed page gratified her.

She approached her new vocation cautiously. She followed
the child protective services piece with one on the town's litter
initiative. The *Sentinel* then came out strongly against a topless bar
that had applied for a liquor permit, a position for which Ed took
some good-natured heat at the golf course. She wrote editorials
pushing raises for public school teachers, opposing a new traffic
pattern in what passed for downtown Centerfield, and
provisionally endorsing an idea to place a security surveillance
camera at an intersection where two fatal accidents had occurred in
a three month span. Ed complimented her, sometimes quoting
comments made to him in praise of the paper's new "relevance."

One afternoon, as she re-wrote her column, Ed appeared in
her doorway.

"Say, Fran, I think I know the answer to this before I ask, but you remember the piece you did on a child protection unit?"

"Sure. It was my first."

"That's the one. The woman in Wall-More—I think you called her Tanya—you changed her name, right? I mean, it wasn't a Tanya that hit the kid and threatened you."

"Her real name is Roberta. Why?"

"Because I got a letter from a lawyer this morning demanding money for his client, Tanya somebody, who says we libeled her. He wants $100,000."

"What lawyer?"

"Arthur Fishburn. I did some checking. He's known around Houston as Arthur Fishbreath."

"That's absurd," Fran said.

"Yeah. It proves you can't be too careful though."

"What are you going to do?"

"I gave it to Rick Lopez, our attorney. He'll write Fishbreath a love note that will say, in essence, 'fuck you, stronger letter to follow,' and that will be the end of it, I hope. And Rick will charge us $500, of course. We better run these by him in advance from now on. As long as we focused on barbeque recipes that seemed unnecessary." Ed turned to leave, then paused. "Why Tanya?"

Fran grinned, as if smiling into a mirror invisible to Ed. The tiny creases at her eyes smiled with her. "Isn't that strange? In the sixth grade I was beat up by a girl named Tanya, and I think I've been looking for revenge ever since."

71

Chapter 26

Fish and Company Smell after
Three Days, and Sometimes Sooner

Arthur Fishburn practiced law from offices on Houston's outer loop. He made his living, an ample living, suing Wall-More. Fishburn & Associates participated in a nationwide network of lawyers and law firms who saw major advantages in always being adverse to a solvent defendant who could pay any judgment rendered. He explained it to newly hired associates, of which there were many, this way: "Think of it as marketing with a twist. Every manufacturer and wholesaler in the world wants shelf space in Wall-More because it gives them instant access to a billion consumers. We want desk space at Wall-More because it gives us access to millions of problems. If one store is screwing up, chances are they are all doing the same thing. It's a system made in class action heaven." Then he would chuckle in that peculiar way of his, which sounded to others like a burp and was frequently accompanied by wafts of purplish vapors from his last meal.

Fishburn preferred spicy foods and expensive haircuts. After one such cut, plastered into semi-permanence by an industrial layer of gel, he thought he noted a resemblance, at a particular angle, to Stephen Segal. This pleased him endlessly, and each month he returned to the stylist with instructions to "make me Segal." Given his height, five feet four inches, and his shape, Bartlett pear with a 46 inch circumference, he favored Stephen Segal to the same degree a German Shepherd favors a goldfish, but the stylist was discreet, not to mention well-tipped, so this absurdity would have passed unnoticed had not Fishburn confided in a secretary whom he felt certain admired him.

"Three guesses," he said to the secretary, who had worked there only two weeks and already had her resume out.

"Oh, Mr. Fishburn, that's unfair," she said. "Give me a hint."

72

Fishburn rubbed his chin, then turned toward her to expose the same angle that had produced the Segal apparition. "How about now?"

"A hint is only fair," she said coyly.

"Okay," he said, a bit impatient that she failed to grasp the obvious. "Action films. Thrillers with lots of violence. Martial arts."

"You know, sir, I never watch those films at all. Not ever. Not even once. I'm the worst person in the world to ask."

"Surely you've seen Stephen Segal."

She stared at him, paralyzed. After several empty seconds she said, "Wow. That's . . . amazing," sincere in a way Fishburn would not have appreciated.

While Wall-More served as Fishburn's professional entree, he also enjoyed salads, hors devours and desserts in the form of spin-offs such as Tanya Carpenter, whose existence on the planet had come to his attention by a time-tested Fishburn process of client acquisition. Fishburn's clipping service furnished him clients the way the yellow pages supplied other lawyers, not that Fishburn & Associates passed up annual full page, color spreads there. He had never heard of the *Sentinel*, much less read it, but he paid his clipping service to send him any article, no matter the content, that mentioned the name "Wall-More." These arrived on a daily basis, and in stupefying quantities. Fishburn himself often culled through them in a process he called "panning for gold." To the untrained ear, these sounded innocent enough--a employee received an award for service, a local charity benefited from a store's donation, a zoning board debated a variance to accommodate a planned construction—but to Fishburn's refined ears these were the opening strains, the overture, to a symphony he called "Cash in C Major." He studied each with a single thought in mind: how can I turn this into a lawsuit. For every employee who received an award, another was excluded; for every charity benefiting from a donation, another went unblessed; for every zoning board asked to re-zone, plenty of people opposed any change; for every Wall-More-related event where a glass stood half full, there might be, if Fishburn looked hard enough, someone holding a glass half empty. That person or organization became Fishburn's friend, and client.

73

Identifying a potential cause of action won a battle, but victory in the war was not declared until Fishburn secured a client. For this he used his network. He sent broadcast e-mails to everyone in the firm, one-hundred twenty lawyers and three-hundred staff, a missive he called "Attention Wall-More Shoppers," specifying the nature of the grievance he had spotted and supplying a general profile of the ideal client. To the employees of Fishburn & Associates, such e-mails represented job advancement opportunities, for it was common knowledge that raises and annual reviews were influenced by tips and referrals leading to the acquisition of clients. In the case of Fran's editorial, Fishburn's shoppers alert had read: "A weekly newspaper called the Centerfield *Sentinel* has defamed a customer named Tanya by reporting a child-beating incident. If anyone knows a Tanya, ask her if she ever frequents W-M with her son, whose name must be Jerome, and find out if she has ever had occasion, while in the store, to reprimand Jerome, but without striking him."

The following day, Fishburn received a referral from a secretary. Upon investigation, he learned that one Tanya Carpenter had recently been to Wall-More with her son Jerome, accompanied by a friend who swore that while she raised her voice to yell at him for putting No. 2 lead pencils up his nose, she did not strike him. Fishburn signed her up, and days later signed the letter Ed Abernathy referred to Rick Lopez for response.

Fishburn labored under no illusions. "It's a nickel-dime case," he told the young associate who had drafted the letter, "but every now and then they write us a check. Or their insurance company writes it. You never know," he said, chuckling in his peculiar way.

Chapter 27

Art takes the Texas Two-step to new lows

Art's check #101, the option on the Travis tract, cleared in two days. OYEVEY's acquisition fund was lighter by one million but the future inhabitants of New Israel were 79 square miles closer to peace and security. Art could hardly believe his good fortune at finding an adjoining tract of 50,000 acres, but before he could contact Rusty Wilson, Wilson called him.

"Mac says you're in the olive business," Wilson said. "Something about worldwide demand for martinis."

"I reckon," Art assured him. "I got new figures this morning. The China market just opened." Art didn't mind disclosing his need for land, as long as his potential sellers remained unaware of the requirement for contiguousness. "I am sorry to hear your wife is ill."

"I 'preciate that. I won't lie, the place has become a bit much to handle. Hope you got lotsa help, cause you're gonna need it."

"When can I see the land?"

"How's next week? Wife's got some tests in Houston so this week is out."

After agreeing to call Wilson the following Monday, Art/Abe hung up. He spread the map on the bed of his motel and carefully delineated the Travis tract in blue ink. A trip to the courthouse the day before had confirmed the boundaries of the Wilson tract, and these he outlined in green. Together, they formed an impressive block of real estate that, while still only a percentage of what was ultimately demanded, could be called a fair beginning. Sitting on the bed, Art felt like Moses, raising his eyes to the remainder of the Promised Land, or in his case the Optioned Land. Records in the courthouse in Centerfield, county seat of Bucko County, confirmed what Art had begun to intuit—that this forsaken expanse of Texas semi-desert offered the perfect mix of sand, dust and dirt, owned by a few rubes who might, with Art's

75

encouragement, be persuaded to retire rich. Art began to take better care of his map, imagining the distant but foreseeable day when it would be the focal point of New Israel's cultural center, sandwiched between sheets of Plexiglas and sealed hermetically in a display case around which school children gathered, and teachers spoke in hushed reverence of the great pioneer Abe Rubiwitz/Art Adams. "On this very map," they would say, "he laid out the vision of New Israel." Art's filigreed boundary lines in blue and green would achieve the mystic consecration of Hancock's signature, da Vinci's drawings, Shakespeare's folios. He envisioned his bust in New I's pantheon of heroes, flanked by prime ministers and benefactors. But first, he must attend a tractor pull.

He'd learned of the event at the county courthouse in Centerfield, where a female deputy clerk with haystack hair and large kaboombas, as his friend Herb called them, chatted up a delivery man restocking the Dr. Pepper machine. "I just love the Durango Destroyer," she said. "When that engine fires up, the vibration makes me horny. I get a big old wide on."

The restocker, whose pocket was graced by an oval patch identifying him as Glenn, took renewed interest at this. "You do, do you? Well, I might just have to bring Cindy with me Saturday night. I damn sure did not know them things was such an afrodisiac."

"Honey, the last one I went to I made Jim Bob take me to the pickup at intermission. Anybody in that parking lot got to see pert near everything there is of me. I told Jim Bob if it embarrassed him, to just go on back to the corn dog stand and I'd meet him there after I took care of some pressing business with his stick shift. If Cindy's anything like me, you better take a fire extinguisher."

Because the colloquialism "hard on" was unknown to Art, he missed her allusion to "wide on," but the stick shift reference was clear enough to anyone from the Middle East or any other point of the globe, so he resolved to see and hear what made the clerk so sexually insistent. Perhaps, if the New I venture failed, he could salvage something by importing this tractor pull to Israel. No shortage of men there could be counted on to escort their ladies to the parking lot at intermission.

He paid ten dollars at the door and bought popcorn. Around him sat men with low slung jeans offering unwanted exposure to the lower sides of their anatomy. Many woman exhibited substantial kaboombas, and Art, a fundamentally proper man, found himself mortified by images of them in contorted pickup abandon. When Defoliator roundly defeated Arizona Fats in a preliminary round, the crowd stood, cheered wildly, and then booed the loser, whose bearded driver waved his middle finger in salute. The engines were impressively loud, but nothing approaching those of the Durango Destroyer, which prowled the ring like some unloosed demon from a Japanese horror movie. It annihilated the Bayou Buttstomper in the featured match. As Art departed, he thought about how those heading with him to the exit would be neighbors to the citizens of New Israel, and the thought pleased him. They were down-to-earth, fun-loving, hard working folk. Best of all, they weren't Arabs.

Art secured Rusty Wilson's 50,000 acres in much the same way he'd negotiated with Mac Travis. Because Travis and Wilson had talked, he got more or less the same terms for more or less the same price. And God knows, he thought after a tour of Wilson's ranch, the land was more or less the same, an unbroken stretch of unbroken stretches. At the end of their third meeting, as Art tendered his check and Wilson signed the option, the name Porkrind Trust again surfaced.

"What is this trust?" Art wished to know.

"Beats hell out of me," Wilson said, slipping Art's check for a million dollars, #102, into his shirt pocket. "All I know is that Porkrind used to own all the land in these here parts. Maybe still owns some. You'd have to check down at the courthouse for that."

Art returned to the courthouse with the dual purpose of inquiring into the trust and eavesdropping on the hay-haired deputy clerk's account of the tractor pull. He entered the deed room to find himself alone with her. She leaned provocatively over an index, her blouse unbuttoned enough to expose an excess of high grade cleavage. One ample hip was slung outward, hugged by a skirt that did not begin to cover her thighs. Having lived in monastic isolation for many weeks, Art could be forgiven his rising expectations. For a moment, she appeared not to be aware of him. He spoiled his view by thudding his folder onto the counter.

"Sorry," she said, looking up. "You been here long?"

"Just arrived," he said. "I'm looking for information about something called the Porkrind Trust."

"Jesus, Mary and Joseph," said the clerk, whose name was Tricksy Faye Dogget. "I've heard of that. What'd you like to know?"

"Mainly, I want to find out if it owns land here."

"Used to own pert near all of Bucko County, I know that much. Been selling, though. Let's check the tax book."

"I don't mean to trouble you."

"Don't you worry 'bout that, honey. It's my job. If I wasn't helping you I'd be sittin' at that desk over yonder, daydreaming about some stud taking me away from all this."

Art smiled politely. "Most kind of you."

Tricksy Faye pulled an oversized book from under the counter. "This is a year or two out of date, but it's a place to start." She ran her finger through an index, then flipped pages until she hit the p's. "Parker, Penneman, Pernell, Pile, Pilgrim, Pitts, Plummer, Porkrind, here it is."

Art eased around beside her, partly to examine the register and mostly because she was leaning again.

"Porkrind still pays taxes on one parcel. Must have sold the rest of it off," she reported. "Looks like maybe 10,000 acres, more or less. Tax bill goes to Austin. Now, if we go over here . . . ." She moved down the counter to another set of books. " . . . we'll see where that parcel is located. She perused the coordinates on the tax plat, then plunked her finger down on spot that drew a gasp from Art. The Porkrind parcel appeared to be surrounded by land he had options on.

Art rubbed his chin. Were he to exercise all his options, the Porkrind piece would be landlocked. Surely that would drive the price down to almost nothing. Porkrind had sold off its other, larger tracts, so maybe it had just forgotten about this one. He relaxed. Ten thousand acres would have set him on acquisitive fire a few months back, but now it sounded hardly worth the effort. A yachtsman pausing to study a row boat. Tricksy Faye moved away from the counter while Art let his eyes follow the motion of her hips.

"Did I see you at the tractor pull Saturday night?" he asked.

"Honey, was you there? If you was there you saw me. I don't miss 'em. I was worried about that Bayou Buttstomper, but it turned out to be just another victim. I hope you didn't have money on that Louisiana thing."

"Me? Oh, no. I like Durango Destroyer."

She pushed the air in front of her with a breezy forward flip of wrist. "You and me both, babe. What I'd give to sit on that driver's lap for thirty minutes." She giggled. "Well, tell the truth I've done that. I know the 'ole boy who drives it."

"What is that like?"

"It's a 600 horse power, gas driven vibrator is what it is. My nips get hard just thinking about it. Say, cowboy, you buyin' or sellin'?"

"Buying," said Art, pleased to be called a cowboy.

"Well, now, any man with that kind of money needs to get to know me, if you catch my drift."

Art wasn't certain what it meant to catch someone's drift. He wondered if her drift might be a sexually transmitted disease.

"Ask me to dinner sometime. I might say yes."

Art studied his hands. He saw himself as a potbellied, un-athletic bystander, long past an age and physique when women her age would serve themselves up for the asking. Not only was he balding on top, but what little hair he had on the rest of his body had turned gray. But now he sensed a rush of testosterone, fueled in part by writing checks in million dollar increments, in part by Tricksy's forthrightness, and by Texas itself, where men spent small fortunes to build machines that ten thousand people paid to watch get returned to scrap metal. Besides, he was lonely. "Would you like to have dinner with me?" he found himself asking.

"Can't tonight," she said. "Hair appointment. How 'bout Friday? After, we can go by the livestock show."

Back at his motel, Art studied his maps, absorbed in his destiny but not unmindful that Friday was only three days away.

Chapter 28

Art's Dreams of Glory Turn Moist

Art rented a convertible for his date with Tricksy. Among the limited things he could think of to make himself younger, that was one. Another was a cologne called Blue Bullet, which he splashed liberally onto his neck and face. When he picked her up, she commented on both before they left her driveway.

She directed him to the Chicken Coop, where she ordered the Cluck Bucket, a platter of assorted parts fried in exotic oils, from peanut to tempura. As they licked their fingers and sipped beer, she asked about his business.

"Olives," she repeated. "You can't mean it. I've never known an olive grower. That's soooo exciting."

"The worldwide olive market is quite dynamic," Art said. "Olive oil is getting long overdue recognition for its health benefits. Demand is outstripping supply."

"I get it," she replied, her big hay-hair bobbing with understanding. "You want to create more supply."

"Precisely," he said.

"Why," she wanted to know, "do they put those little red thingies in them? I don't care for the little red thingies. I pick them out."

"Spanish olives. Those are pimentos."

"Is that what they are?" She laughed, then seemed to turn serious. "You know how they make grapes now without seeds?"

"Yes."

"Well, why can't they do that for olives? You know, breed them so they don't have any pits."

"I'm not sure," Art said. "Maybe someone is working on that."

In the Chicken Coop's parking lot, she took his hand as they walked to the car. "You're gonna luv this livestock show," she

80

promised. In the car, she again took his hand, sliding it into her lap. He was glad now he'd opted for the automatic.

At the livestock show she led him from exhibit to exhibit, barn to barn. She knew details about rabbits, turkeys, sheep, pigs, and goats. In particular she knew the breeding habits of each, and when she described their couplings her voice took on a tone faintly professorial, as if her authority was not subject to challenge. "The goats are the worst," she told him. "Nasty boys, those billy goats. When they're not beating off they're giving each other blow jobs. If I was a lady goat I wouldn't stand for it. Let's go see the big boys."

By big boys, she meant the bulls and stallions. "My, my," she said as they paused at a corral. "Look at the hammer on that bad boy." A stallion stood twenty feet away, his substantial penis extending toward the floor. Art gazed at the horse's head, then at her, and finally allowed his eyes to come to rest on the object of her interest. An interest which, he learned over the course of the next hour, came closer to being, and was accurately described as, an obsession. At the stall of an enormous bull, she lingered, unwilling to move, for a full twenty minutes. "Poor baby. I think he's shy. He's keeping things private."

"Well," said Art, "perhaps we should respect his privacy." He pulled at her gently but she refused to budge.

"He'll come out," she said, meaning IT would come out. "Sooner or later he'll have to pee, and no bull is gonna pee with his hammer inside." Her patience was rewarded, and as she had predicted, the benighted animal soon felt nature's call. From beneath his hind legs a dark tumescence emerged, and kept emerging, unwinding like a fireman's hose, until it almost touched the floor.

Tricksy gasped audibly. "My savior in heaven, can you believe THAT!" She turned to him as if her question was not rhetorical. "Just think of the poor cow that sees that coming at her."

Art became conscious of a physical phenomena that had begun at the first stallion's corral. He felt himself contracting, shriveling as though he had been plunged into a cold ocean, his scrotum reduced in size by half and his quite modest member, such as it was, foreshortened to invisibility. He began to wonder if it was possible for his genitals to retract into their pre-partum position.

81

He turned his thoroughly inadequate face to her as she said, "Just imagine the shot that old boy fires when that rifle goes off." He urged her away, her eyes still riveted on the bull's elongated schlong, but instantly regretted his decision when they arrived at the next corral.

"Hot damn," she said, wide-eyed. "A boner." It was true. A midnight black stallion stood in an undeniable state of arousal, his mighty sword swashbuckling under his belly as he attempted to rear up, constrained by lead lines. "He smells it," she said, smirking. "Something close is in heat. Jesus, maybe it's me."

At the car, Art slumped gratefully into his seat, happy to be rid of comparisons unflattering to his ego, even if he was the only one making them. And he couldn't be sure he was.

His relief was short lived. Tricksy leaned across the console, kissed him full on the lips, and placed her right hand precisely on his zipper. "Bet you can't guess what I'm in the mood for," she said, nuzzling him.

He cleared his throat pointedly, afraid to speak for fear of singing the kind of falsetto note appropriate to the castrato he now felt himself to be. "Well . . . ," he finally managed.

Her living room redefined American kitsch for Art. Over her couch, a framed velvet tiger sprawled in situ, jungle greenery clashing at every turn with the colors of the cat. They did not, however, pause at the couch, Tricksy pulling him physically into the bedroom at a speed that did not permit leisurely survey of her home. On a low table in one corner, a collection of Barbie dolls reclined. Over the pillow-strewn waterbed, Cheerleader Tricksy gave an 11 X 14 mid-air yell for the home team, BHS emblazoned on her sweater and her legs spread in athletic gambol. Standing by the bed unbuttoning her blouse, she said, "You just think of me as your little heifer, here to make her bull happy."

Art sat on the bed, bobbing slightly with the undulating water and watching as she shed her clothes. "Yes, well about the bull . . . ."

She slipped her panties off, tossing them on the Barbie table with a flick of her foot. She stood naked before him, her breasts as ample as the cheerleader's, a generous triangle of blonde pubic hair matted from the just-relieved press of the panties. "Now that's what I call comfort," she said. "Here, I'll help you get comfortable."

Making Art comfortable was not going to be easy. He had begun to sense nausea from the motion of the waterbed, his stomach sending up an unwelcome "ahoy, mate!" to reaffirm his lifelong proneness to seasickness. Worse, he felt the onset of a panic attack centered on any attempt to locate his penis. He doubted he himself could find it, and her hunt, certain to be futile, shrank him further. As she reached for his belt buckle, he caught her hand.

"Your bull needs a little more time in the pasture," he said.

She sat beside him, extended one arm over his shoulder, and said, "I understand. Sometimes I come on a bit strong. How about a nice massage?"

Anything to buy time, thought Art, so he helped her remove his shirt. At her direction he lay prone, face down on the bed. She straddled him at the waist and began kneading his shoulders. Beneath him the wavelets of the waterbed ebbed and flowed. He relaxed. This was quite nice. When she bent to reach his biceps, he could feel her breasts brush across his back in a pleasurable swish. On her next extension he felt pressure on his back from her pubis bone, cushioned by the downy mons. He sensed a stirring below, life seeping into his missing member, the urban guerilla coming out of hiding. He rolled over. She stared down at him. "Feeling better?" she asked.

"Much better."

She thrust her hips upward, as if he had pinched her. "I'll say we're feeling better. I think the bull is ready for the rodeo."

"It's not much of a bull," he said. "Just to warn you, it's pretty small. And I haven't had sex since my wife died four years ago. I'll probably embarrass myself."

"That's okay, honey" she said tenderly. "I've got my own problems in the you-know-what department."

In that she had not failed to mention the "what" of any what they had encountered, he said, "No, I don't know what. What?"

"Oh, you know. The "o" word."

"Oprah?"

"Close. Orgasm. I like to look at the animals to get me primed, so to speak. I wouldn't want to disappoint a big, handsome cowboy like yourself."

He returned the smile. "You couldn't disappoint me."

She leaned far over, resting her breasts on either side of his face.

"Why don't you see if you can find the bull," he said.

She found it, lassoed it and led it where it needed to go. Later, as they showered, she bent down to examine his sated member. "Hey, where's your helmet?"

"What helmet?"

"All the guys I've been with have a helmet on their salamis. Yours is bareheaded."

"That's because I've been circumcised. I'm Jewish."

"Well, fuck me sideways. I never seen one like that. Kinda cute. Did it hurt?"

"No."

Chapter 29

Cricket, Anyone?

Fran cursed Ed Abernathy, but did so under her breath as Sarah, Chip and James were in the car with her. "I can't believe I'm actually driving to Albuquerque to see a doctor."

"Just this once, Fran," Ed had assured her. "You need to go one time so they can open charts on everyone. Then you'll have your primary care physician and get referrals to Houston specialists for real problems. Trust me on this. I'll pay for the gas and hotel. Hell, we'll pay your salary for the days you're gone. Take the kids to see some mesa out there. Turn it into a short, paid holiday."

The trip gave James a chance to vent, yet again, his frustration with his high school football team, the Centerfield Cougars, currently the holder of the longest losing streak in the state in its division. James played wide receiver, a position suited to the long, rangy build he had inherited from his father. The problem continued to be Lionel, James insisted. Lionel was the coach. When it opened, Centerfield High had been too small and remote to attract an experienced coach in the competitive fervor of Texas high school football, so had settled for a soccer coach, a Brit, to whom American football remained something of a mystery. Lionel stressed sportsmanship, some said because he lacked the knowledge and experience to stress things like blocking and tackling, but in this area he was a tyrant. While their opponents screamed epithets about the Cougars' mothers, their sisters and even their grandmothers, the Cougars were required, on penalty of being benched, to retort with phrases like "good show" and "well done." Lionel had been there for two decades now, still urging his "lads" to give "full effort" on Friday nights. A rumor had it that Centerfield High would soon start a soccer team, to which it hoped to transition Lionel, but any such move would likely come too late to help James, who had begun to wonder if they would win a game before he graduated.

Fran found a Super 6 Motel outside of Albuquerque and took two rooms. The next morning she drove to her appointment. A gleaming new glass and steel building housed the Big Toe HMO. No one could explain the source of the name, although one nurse quipped ominously that it derived from the only body part fully covered by the plan. For an hour Fran filled out forms. An hour after that, a nurse announced that Dr. Punjabi would see her.

Dr. Punjabi stood five feet, one inch tall, counting the turban. He wore a broad smile, said little, and spent fifteen minutes examining Fran, and the same amount of time examining each child. By eleven a.m. they prepared to leave.

Fran approached the nurse. "I didn't want to be rude," Fran said. "What language is Dr. Punjabi speaking?"

"English," said the nurse. "I should have warned you. He's still having trouble with some vowels."

And some consonants, Fran thought but did not say.

Chapter 30

That's Why They Pay Him the Big Money

Arthur Fishburn tossed Rick Lopez's letter aside, having read only the opening sentence. He knew from experience what would follow. And, for once, he rejoiced in rejection, because as a result of a rare malfunction in the well-oiled machine that was Fishburn & Associates, he now hunted bigger game.

Fishburn's system for client recruitment, by which Tanya Carpenter had been secured, demanded an e-mail to staff alerting them to the fact that the office had now obtained the sought for individual and the staff could turn its attention to other matters. For some reason—Fishburn would investigate—no such e-mail circulated after Tanya Carpenter retained the firm. As a result, the staff continued its quest for the ideal client. They e-mailed the results to Fishburn.

"Yikes!" said Fishburn as he read responses. "Twenty-eight Tanyas who abuse kids named Jerome in Wall-More! And that's just in Houston!" He did some rough math. "Nationwide, there must be over 50,000 of them. I'm smelling class action!"

"I'm confused," said his associate. "A weekly newspaper won't have money to pay a big award, even with insurance."

"That's why we'll also sue Wall-More," Fishburn said.

"What did Wall-More do?"

"Why . . . nothing!" Fishburn stammered. "That's the point. Wall-More did nothing while this went on in their stores. They negligently and with gross disregard for their customers, our 50,000 clients named Tanya, did absolutely nothing."

"Maybe I'm dense," said the associate, "but I still don't see how that subjects Wall-More to liability."

"I'll think of something," Fishburn said, chuckling in his peculiar way.

Chapter 31

Putting Without Ed

Kirstin leaned forward, turned her head in the direction of the armadillo's mouth, struck her pink ball firmly, then watched it undulate along the carpet, through the yawning armadillo, and just wide of the cup.

"Nice shot," Fran said. With putter in hand, she approached the tee. "Here goes nothing." Her shot ricocheted off the armadillo's tongue, sending her down a blind alley from which two shots would be a minimum. Putt-putt golf had been Kirstin's idea.

Kirstin tapped in, retrieved her ball, and turned to offer Fran advice. "Aim for the left cheek," she advised.

Fran's ball struck a wall six inches from her point of aim, caroming back to within inches of where she started. "I'm not much good at this."

"You've never played," Kirstin said.

On the next hole, Fran cleanly cleared an oil derrick and scored a two. Kirstin clapped encouragement. For the next half-hour they wove their way through, under, around and over The Alamo, a giant cactus, a long horn steer, and other assorted obstacles. They had the course to themselves. Kirstin mentioned therapy.

"How goes it?" Fran asked.

"It's hard. I guess I'm making progress. All this childhood stuff she wants me to talk about. I think she wants me to see that some of this isn't all my fault. This week she mentioned bringing my parents in for a session or two."

Fran looked up from her putt. "That's often done. It could be interesting." She swung the club, sending the ball smartly toward a border checkpoint. "How are classes going?"

"Fine, except it's hard to study with all the construction. I don't see why Dad needs an Irish Pub, but it's his money."

"What does he say?"

"He says it will be good exercise. He's putting in a dart board. Lots of walking back and forth, he says." Kirstin placed her ball down. "What's this I hear about you stepping out?" She grinned at her ball instead of Fran.

Fran laughed lightly. "Sounds like Sarah has been blabbing. I've been out with him a couple of times. He's harmless."

"Flowers?"

"Why, that little snitch. I need to speak to Sarah about gossip."

"I've told you things," Kirstin said. "A few details won't hurt."

"I guess you're right," Fran said, smiling. "Let's see. . . a few details. Well, his name is Todd Melville, he's pretty wealthy from what I've heard, but fortunately that hasn't come from him. He's attractive, I suppose. Divorced, no children." Fran hoped she would not ask where they had met. COUGH would never be a fun subject.

"Where is his ex?"

"Dallas. He doesn't talk about her much, to my great relief."

"Do you know her name?"

"He mentioned it. It's one of those double names Southerners like so much. Nan Tucker."

"What's she like?"

"My, you're curious."

"Aren't you?"

"Okay, a little," Fran said. They had stopped playing. Fran leaned on her club, facing Kirstin across the Rio Grande. "She must be something of a loner. Keeps to herself, Todd says. Very inward. He doesn't criticize her for it, but reading between the lines it must have caused some problems, because he's so outgoing."

"What about that 'opposites attract' thing?"

"There's something to it. Jim, my husband, loved the outdoors. He would have slept outdoors if I had agreed. I'm an inside person. Give me a book and a lamp and a comfortable chair and I'm in heaven. And we got along great."

"I've seen his picture at your house," Kirstin said. "He was like really good looking."

Fran smiled distantly. "Yes. I miss him. The kids miss him."

"It doesn't seem fair."

"Many things in life are not. For example, it doesn't seem fair that it should take me three times as many shots to get this ball in that little cup."

Kirstin said, "I guess you're just going to be one of life's losers," at which they both laughed until Fran felt at risk for wetting her pants.

Chapter 32

*Rick Explains Fishburn's Offensive,
to which Ed Takes Offense*

On the morning the U.S. Marshall served the class action suit on Ed, Rick Lopez had only one time slot in his appointment calendar, forcing Ed to cancel his golf match for the first time in recent memory.

They met in Rick's office, a wood paneled cave with pictures of foxhunting everywhere. Rick sat behind a large desk covered with paper. On the floor behind him, files stood in piles. He read the Complaint while Ed gazed at depictions of hounds and hunters.

"The slimy bastard," Rick muttered. "Fifty-thousand Tanyas. Absurd."

Ed pretended to study a horse clearing a jump, his back to Rick. "At least we have company, although it's hard for me to see what Wall-More did wrong."

"Hell, it's hard to see what anyone did wrong. This lawsuit is mindless bullshit. Hasn't this guy Fishburn ever heard of the First Amendment?"

"Evidently not," Ed said, trying to remember exactly how the First Amendment factored in.

"We'll counterclaim. This is abuse of process."

"I'm not sure what that is," Ed admitted, "but I like the sound of it."

Rick said, "Ed, stop pacing and sit down. I want to be clear on the facts. Some woman on your editorial staff witnessed a big momma working her kid over in Wall-More, am I right?"

"Correct-o," Ed said.

"And was her name Tanya?"

"Roberta."

"Now how do you know that?"

"Because Fran, my assistant editor, checked with the store. The woman shops there and this wasn't the first time she beat on one of her kids." As Rick again studied the Complaint, Ed realized that he had never before referred to Fran as an assistant editor.

"What about the kid?" Rick asked. "Was his name Jerome?"

Ed sighed. "That part is true. Fran changed the mother's name, but she used the kid's real name. It didn't seem to matter since the mother wasn't identified."

"Makes sense to me," Rick acknowledged.

"Are we in deep do-do?" Ed asked.

Rick extended his eyeglasses to the tip of his nose, peering over them. "Truth is a complete defense to libel," he said, "but your editorial is only partly true; the Jerome part."

"It's all true. We changed the mugger's name to protect her."

"I know that, and you know that, and had you called me prior to printing it I would have advised you to do exactly what you did. But this guy Fishburn is claiming that by protecting Roberta, you've defamed Tanya—fifty-thousand of them."

"So some Tanya in St. Louis who beat her kid in Wall-More can sue a weekly newspaper in Texas?

"Anyone can sue anybody. And the wire services ran the story, so folks in St. Louis read about it."

"What did Wall-More do?"

"It says here they knowingly and intentionally aided and abetted a member of the news media to invade the parental bonds of customers, thereby infringing on the civil rights of women named Tanya to discipline their children named Jerome. They're alleging conspiracy."

"But that makes no sense."

"Welcome to my world," Rick said.

Chapter 33

Fran Streps Over the Line, Receives Culture Shock

Fran knew that her new insurance would be tested sooner rather than later. The test came when Sarah developed a sore throat that Fran suspected of being strep. She placed a long distance call to Albuquerque. A nurse answered.

"This is Angela Morris," the nurse said. "How can I help you?"

Fran explained the symptoms.

"You need to bring her in," Angela said.

"I can't. I'm in Centerfield. That's in Texas."

"Our guidelines say she must be seen."

Fran felt her blood pulsing in her temples. "I had this discussion with Dr. Punjabi when I brought Sarah for her physical. That was just a month ago. I told him we live in another state and that I wouldn't be able to bring her eight hundred miles for routine sicknesses. He said, 'No problem,' or at least I think that's what he said."

"Dr. Punjabi is new," Angela explained. "He probably wasn't aware of the policy."

"What will he do if I bring her there?"

"It depends on the test results."

"I've had three kids," Fran said, unable to keep irritation out of her tone. "I know he'll swab her throat, and I can't drive eight hundred miles to get that done. Can't you just refer me to someone in Houston who can do a throat culture? It only takes twelve seconds."

"I don't think we can do that," Angela said. "But it does seem like a long way to drive. I'll check with our administrator and call you back."

"Will that be today?"

"It's flu season. But I'll try to get an answer promptly."

"Thank you," Fran said, hanging up.

93

Fran did not hear from Angela, or Dr. Punjabi, and by late afternoon Sarah had not improved. Fran carried her to Quick Fix MDs, a minor emergency care center on the outskirts of Houston. She paid $185 for the visit, a throat culture, and a prescription, thinking all the while about how she would present the bills to Ed for reimbursement.

Chapter 34

Civil War II

Each July Centerfield sponsored Buster Bustamonte Day, a three day festival honoring its namesake. They closed off Main Street at noon on Friday, to give the carnival acts and food vendors time to set up. By evening, Mariachi bands played, beer flowed, citizens danced, old people held hands, and middle-aged women waited for Buster to appear on the balcony of the town hall, doff his baseball cap, and shoot into the air an ancient revolver his great-great-grandfather had fired in the service of Santa Anna. The pistol shot technically violated a town ordinance against discharging firearms, but no one aware of the violation cared. On Saturday, fireworks commenced at dawn, followed by daylong celebrations fueled by alarming amounts of beer, wine and tequila. At three p.m. a parade turned each corner of the town square before heading west, toward Buster's hacienda, where Buster mingled with the crowd, signed autographs, and oversaw the provision of punch and candy to the marchers. After sunset, young girls locked arms to walk the square, avoiding the prying stares of young boys, who circled them in the opposite direction. At ten, another fireworks display exploded above the square, its most brilliant flashes illuminating, for only an instant, the young boys and girls whose eyes had met in the promenade, and who now found a few moments of privacy in the cleft of a doorway or the unobserved side of a tree.

Saturday's festivities foreshadowed the undisputed main event of every Bustamonte Day, the barbeque cook-off, held on Sunday. As many as two hundred contestants arose at dawn to begin smoking their entries. Some of these missed church for the first and last time all year. In addition to matchless prestige, the winner received two game tickets to Buster's personal box at the stadium, plus the privilege of cooking his or her award winning entry for Buster and his extended family, which last year had numbered eighty-three.

The Bustamonte Barbeque awarded one prize, making it unique among contests with penchants for silver metals, runners up, and other recognition systems designed to send losers home with salvaged pride. At Bustamonte Day, the winner walked away with the entire gilded taco while everyone else planned for next year.

An award carrying such implications could not be left to the opinion of one judge. A three member panel decided the winner. Two judges had to come from Texas--that provision had been foresightedly inserted into the town's charter. The organizing committee selected the third judge from a roster of barbeque experts in states ranging from Texas to Oklahoma. This year, a rancher from Tulsa had been invited and had accepted. His pedigree included winning a recent competition in Oklahoma and bottling his own private label sauce. His participation appeared to assure the most discerning standard for excellence until . . .

Until a good citizen of Centerfield who happened to be an annual contestant and perpetual loser of the competition went onto the internet to do some checking. There, to his shock, he learned that Brock Rutledge, the Tulsa rancher, had been born and grew up in New Hampshire. At this revelation, the chitlins hit the fan, the bovine fur flew, the snout had to shout, and Ed Abernathy, sitting at his table on the nineteenth hole, said "kiss my cactus" at least five times.

Letters poured in to the *Sentinel*. Ed read Fran excerpts from his favorites.

> It would be a tragedy of the highest magnitude if our two Texas judges, split in their views and seduced by the savory loins of competing sows, were forced to turn to somebody from New Hampshire to decide the winner. We might just as well draw straws, because we can have no confidence in the opinion of some New England Minute Man who wouldn't know a hog from a hacksaw or barbeque from a baboon. Signed: Lester Smidlapp."

96

Or this:

> It is not in my Christian soul to condemn a man I
> have never met, but I will lay anyone in our fair
> township thirty-to-one odds that this man, Brock
> Rutledge, is a vinegar man. Oh, he will talk tomato-
> base, and he may have even used catsup to hide his
> true colors, but in his heart of hearts he is a heathen
> vinegar-baser. Cast him out before swine. Signed:
> Mona Urgahart.

Fran laughed. "I assume you'll cover our position on this
one."

Ed nodded with an air of destiny. "I was born to write this
editorial."

Chapter 35

Fran Learns What She Already Knows

A week after taking Sarah to Quick Fix MDs, Fran received a letter from Big Toe HMO. "Thank you for using our laboratory facilities. Your test has been analyzed by our staff and the results show conclusively that you are/are not pregnant." The "are not" had been circled. She placed a long distance call to Angela Morris.

"Angela no longer works here," she heard a much too cheery voice say. "I'm Rosetta Aldama, and I will be happy to help you."

Fran explained her call about Sarah's throat culture. "There's been some kind of error," she said. "I just received test results from a test I never took."

"What kind of results?"

"Pregnancy."

"Oh, you're pregnant?"

"Not unless the laws of nature have been repealed, and I haven't been tested either. I only called to get a test authorized for my daughter."

"A lot of women say that."

"Say what?"

"That the test is for their daughter."

"It was a strep test, and my daughter is five. I never heard from anyone with Big Toe HMO, so I took care of it. I'm only calling now to alert you to some mix-up in your lab because I received these results for a test I never took. In other words, someone out there is waiting for the results mistakenly sent to me."

"Who is your doctor?"

"Dr. Punjabi. Your computer should have a note of my call."

"The computers are down, and Dr. Punjabi is at the mosque. I'll make sure he gets this message."

"Don't forget," Fran admonished. "I know what it's like to hang in the breeze for test results."

"I won't forget. Excuse me, there's another call. Goodbye."

As the dial tone hummed, Fran thought: the mosque?

Chapter 36

Chip, A Hip and a Skip

On the second surgery to repair Chip's severely broken hip, doctors had inserted a titanium pin, which each morning set off the metal detector at his school. The policeman on duty automatically shunted him to a holding area, where an assistant principal would scan his pants with a hand-held detector. The policeman assigned to Bustamonte Junior High knew Chip, knew the source of the alarming beep, and apologized for having to delay his arrival in class with such a pointless routine, but claimed he had no choice under the very tightly controlled security dictated by the school board. When Chip had first entered the school, Fran had applied for a waiver, but was turned down with the explanation that no student could be exempted for any reason, and while the metal pin in his hip did not present a direct threat to student safety, it offered a miscreant (not that her son was one, the board emphasized) a cover for the guns, knives, and explosive devices at which the detectors were aimed. Bustamonte Junior High, the board had concluded with a flourish, maintained a "zero tolerance" for weapons.

During Chip's first year at the school, Mr. Parker, an assistant principal, conducted the hand-held scans. He also conducted the strip searches and body cavity searches for boys suspected of carrying drugs. Each morning he pointed the unit's antenna at Chip's hip, listened for the confirmatory beep, and waved him through.

In this year, Chip's second, Mr. Parker was replaced by a female gym teacher named Ms. Heckmon. When Chip asked what happened to Mr. Parker, Ms. Heckmon explained that he had resigned over the summer to take a job with the Texas penal system, which paid him more to do essentially the same work. The last Ms. Heckmon had heard, he had been assigned to the Austin Outhouse,

100

a pejorative attached to the youth center for teens convicted of killing their families (three member minimum).

The assistant principals conducted their searches in a small office off the main entrance. In the third week of school, Chip found himself alone in this office with Ms. Heckmon, who seemed to take a greater interest in him than on previous mornings.

"How do I know that you're not hiding something in your pants?" she asked.

Chip said, "It's just the pin. I swear. Same as yesterday."

"But how can I be sure? A big, strong, good-looking boy like you could be hiding anything in there." She approached him with her wand.

Chip averted his eyes. "Really, it's just the pin."

She looked toward the door. "I have a job to do. I think I need to be sure."

"How?"

"Well, suppose you drop your pants."

Chip's face grew flush. "I don't think I should."

"You hiding something?"

"No."

"My little magic box says you are." She passed the hand-held in front of his eyes, still averted. "You could be hiding something in there. Something that could threaten school safety. It's my job to check it out." She stood next to him.

Chip cleared his throat. "I don't think you should. I need to go now. Have a nice day, Ms. Heckmon." He left without looking back.

Chapter 37

Ed Plots an Offensive Defense without Being Defensive

The class action filed by Arthur Fishburn on behalf of Tanya Carpenter "and fifty-thousand Tanyas similarly situated" presented the *Sentinel* with a classic editorial dilemma. Fran asked Ed if she could write the story.

"What story?"

"Ed, we've got to report it."

"They sued us. Why should we?"

"Because we're a newspaper and it's our responsibility to report the news, good or bad."

"It's Fishbreath's responsibility to take his pound of flesh out of someone else."

"So maybe we say that, but we have to say something."

"I don't know. Let me think it over. I'll call you from the golf course."

Ed kept his word. He called that afternoon after several rounds at the nineteenth hole. Fran gathered he was not alone.

"Hey, Frannie," he yelled over a surrounding din.

Fran moved her head several inches from the receiver. "Yes, Ed?"

"Hey, Frannie. You still think we need to give Fishbreath some free publicity."

"We don't have to mention his name."

"The hell we don't. I want every swinging dick and tit in Centerfield to know just what a slimeball this guy is."

"Ed, you're on a cell phone, so perhaps you want to be more careful about what you say. You're also quite drunk."

"Frannie, Frannie, you're a plain talkin' old girl, aren't you?"

"I can be direct when I need to be."

"Well, I want you to be the most direct you've ever been when you write this up. I want to be so direct that Fishbreath will go direct to his window to pull the blinds so he won't have to face

102

our readers, and then I want him to go direct to the bathroom to pee in his pants when he realizes what we're going to do to his greasy little money machine."

"What are we going to do to his greasy little money machine?"

"We're going to get our favorite mechanic, one Richard V. Rick Lopez, attorney at law, to throw the biggest wrench he can lift and counter-sue his ass from here to Toledo. Then we're going to—"

Fran hung up. She re-read the Complaint, made some notes, then began outlining her column. She had reached a rough mid-point when the phone rang. Rosetta Aldama of the Big Toe HMO regretted to inform her that her request for a strep culture had been denied, but that out of concern for its patients, our "family" she called it, Big Toe HMO would be automatically reviewing the decision, and she would be notified of the results in two to four weeks. Fran's representation that Sarah had been treated and cured several weeks before was interrupted by a call Rosetta regrettably had to take.

Chapter 38

All Passengers Who Missed the Post-Luncheon Buffet
Report to the Libido Deck for a Pre-Dinner Snack

Construction continued on the Fafalones' addition. The Irish Pub began to take shape, Joyce's solarium awaited tiles imported from Mexico, and delays imparted to the spa the cache of a room that would never be finished or, if finished, never used. George and Joyce decided to take a cruise to escape banging hammers.

Joyce voiced her concerns about leaving Kirstin and Scott alone for ten days. For one thing, she had recently heard what sounded like running followed by giggling upstairs, which caused her to question whether Allison had come over to study, as Scott claimed. George reminded her that Scott was nearly old enough to vote. When the voice of Joyce admitted this was true, they decided on the Aegean Sea. Joyce left instructions in a note posted by magnet to the refrigerator. "While we are gone, you must follow these rules: (1) no parties during the week; (2) no overnight visitors unless we know them; (3) do not drive the Mercedes except in emergencies; (4) watch the videos I left on the console." The videos were *Cool Hand Luke*, *Amadeus*, and *The Pelican Brief*. She had searched for, but had been unable to find, the film she called *Twelve Grown Men* because she thought it taught important lessons about jumping to conclusions, and because Lee J. Cobb reminded her of George. When she mentioned this to George in the middle of the Aegean Sea, he told her that the film she had in mind was *Twelve Angry Men* and it was no surprise she couldn't find it as no one who worked in the video store had been born when it was made. Yes, it was shameful how little young people knew about great films and no, he did not think it necessary to send Scott an e-mail recommending it.

George and Joyce took full advantage of the luxuries offered on board ship. They ate five meals a day on sea days and added a sixth on port days, when they could make lunch or dinner reservations at a fine local restaurant. George tipped generously because the thinness of waiters demonstrated how difficult life must be in whatever country they were in, and he liked the fact that after these local meals they sometimes walked several blocks for sightseeing, by which he got his exercise. Notwithstanding such exercise, and in spite of his resolution to eat at least one helping of fruit with lunch, George gained twelve pounds in the first few days at sea. He joked with Joyce that soon he would be unable to fit into the new size fifty-six shorts she had gifted to him for the cruise and she joked with him that she was more concerned about his health than his shorts. They enjoyed a good laugh over this repartee until he began to cough violently, at which she was about to summon a steward when he managed to clear the cocktail onion that had almost clogged his windpipe.

The cruise proved unusual in that the Fafalones did not meet another couple with whom they bonded, as they had on the only other cruise they had taken, eight years earlier. George reported with obvious disappointment that those he met at dinner or on the tanning deck did not seem that interested in the funeral business. At the Star Browser Lounge one evening he met a man with whom he felt certain he would find rapport because the stranger mentioned suicidal feelings. George bought him countless drinks but, as George related to Joyce the morning after, the man had shown himself to be a bore by talking about his will to live.

Joyce found better luck at the massage tables, where she met a woman about her age who seemed nice. Her name was Nora. Nora told Joyce that she had noticed Joyce and George in the buffet line and had assumed they were married.

"Oh, yes," confirmed Joyce, "twenty-six years next month."

"You're so lucky," said Nora, who spoke through her nose. "George reminds me of my Harry, may God rest his soul."

"Is Harry dead?" Joyce asked.

Nora nodded. "Last year. He had a heart attack just after we got home from this same cruise. I found him face down in the herb garden, gasping for breath. I panicked, I suppose, because I didn't call 911 as quickly as I might have—I was trying to make him comfortable and to get him to talk to me—oh, it was horrible, and then when I finally did reach 911 they couldn't find the house right away, so there was more delay. I laid his head in my lap, in the row between the rosemary and the cilantro, and he died right then, in my arms. I thought coming back to sea, where we had so many nice memories, would help me adjust, don't you know."

Joyce noticed tears in her eyes, then said, "I know we just met, but may I ask you a very personal question?"

With a certain intimacy Nora told Joyce she could ask anything—that she felt better having someone to share her grief with.

"Does my George remind you of Lee J. Cobb, the actor?"

"No," Nora said.

"That's so funny. George reminds me of Lee J. Cobb."

Chapter 39

On Today's Spot Market, Forty Acres
and a Mule Will be Expensive

Todd Melville invited Fran to a meeting of SNEEZE, largely to impress her with the breadth of his interests. He felt his introduction to her as a member of COUGH had set the wrong tone for the relationship he now hoped to encourage, even though Fran had no recollection of having met him there. At SNEEZE he would be seen as a leader of forward thinking instead of a follower of dogma.

Melville believed that the group's commitment to ZEN EMPHASIS put the organization on a higher intellectual plateau than conventional think tanks such as the Brookings Institute and the NRA. It mandated a circular table, to give all participants an equal voice, a requirement that complicated meeting logistics because the Longhorn Room at the only Holiday Inn in Centerfield would accommodate only a small circular table allowing a maximum of twelve. For the meeting Fran attended, this problem was rendered manageable by the attendance of seven people.

Melville called the meeting to order. "Today, we will debate the issue of reparations for slavery. As you know, this idea is being increasingly advanced by some as a way of righting what most advanced thinkers consider a terrible injustice. I hope you all read the material circulated in advance of today's meeting. I've asked my friend Fran to join us today. In addition to being the mother of three, she writes editorials for the *Sentinel*, which I'm sure all of us here read weekly." The group extended polite applause, which Fran acknowledged with a quick smile.

A man with thick glasses and a NASA pocket protector spoke. "Mr. Chairman, I have looked forward to this discussion. If it is anything like our last meeting on opening the border between Texas and Mexico, we're in for an entertaining afternoon. I wonder, though, if we should not have at least one black person here."

"An excellent point, Mr. Flask. You'll be pleased to learn I have invited just such a person. She should arrive at any moment. Until she does, I'd like some comments on the reading materials."

Ten minutes into the discussion, Rachel Robinson arrived. She apologized for being held up by a construction delay outside Houston, her home. She was slim, early fifties, and neatly dressed in a dark suit not common to women in Centerfield. Melville introduced her as a professor of sociology at Rice.

"Professor Robinson, may we call you Rachel?" Melville asked.

"Please do," she said.

"Rachel, I know you've studied this issue. Give us your thoughts."

Rachel Robinson spoke softly in a manner that resulted in listeners breathing quietly so as to hear all she said. She confessed that she had been skeptical of the reparations idea until the U.S. had agreed to award them to Japanese Americans displaced by internment during World War II. What blacks had suffered paled internment by comparison, she told them. She had not yet decided on an amount that would be appropriate, nor the precise method of compensation, but she thought debate about such issues should be part of any resolution once the principle of reparations had been adopted.

A woman sitting beside Flask asked the first question. "I am from Mexican decent," she said. "My ancestors were not slaves, but they might as well have been given their treatment. Should we be entitled to reparations?"

Rachel responded calmly that the difference between being slaves and "might as well have been" was oceanic, and while she had no doubt that Mexicans had been mistreated and suffered deprivations, she did not consider the situations comparable.

A man who identified himself as Bruce Bulkington spoke next. He said that his ancestry was Native American, and that if anyone had a beef with White America it was "my tribe." He expressed sympathy for Rachel's cause, but wondered if his was not more compelling.

Rachel agreed that Native Americans had suffered injustice on a scale with Black Americans and that reparations were indeed appropriate for them. This pleased Bulkington, whose business was real estate and who expressed interest in being on the team that renegotiated the price of Manhattan, "not to mention Ohio, Illinois and the Great Lakes." Rachel took this sarcasm in stride, suggesting that justice was often expensive.

Fran remained silent until Todd Melville asked her opinion. "I agree that reparations are justified," she said, "but if I were black I wouldn't want them."

"Why not?" Rachel Robinson asked.

"Because in the 1960s the country undertook a great humanitarian gesture called welfare, and I can't think of anything short of cocaine addiction that has done more damage to black and white alike."

Rachel Robinson eyed her steadily. "My family was on welfare once when I was young. It's the only reason I'm where I am today."

"So was mine," Fran said, "and it tore us apart in ways we'll never get over."

Chapter 40

Fran is Reminded of Why She Doesn't Own a TV

While George and Joyce ate their way across the Aegean, Kirstin asked Fran over. They sat on Kirstin's bed, talking in a way that each had come to enjoy. Mostly, Fran listened as Kirstin worked her way around a number of obstacles that many women her age had already navigated. Fran took pride in Kirstin's evident determination to do what Kirstin called "get serious."

Kirstin reported that she had begun to enjoy her psychology class. At the local community college, she felt at home among students that, for various reasons, pursued education at an alternative pace. One such student, Amber, shared her taste in music and her off-beat sense of humor. Amber came from a background and neighborhood not unlike Kirstin's, and, like Kirstin, the chance to go to a traditional four-year college had been but one more expensive gift discarded casually into a corner. "We even look alike," Kirstin said. "It's spooky."

"So things are going well," said Fran.

Kirstin hesitated. "Pete is a problem."

"You're not seeing him again, are you?"

"Yes, but in a way that's creepy."

"What do you mean?"

"I think he's stalking me. I can't be sure, but the last two times I've come out of psychology, I could swear he's been waiting in the parking lot."

"On the motorcycle?"

"No. A blue truck I've never seen him drive. I might be wrong, but I have like this bad feeling. And I've been getting hang-up calls."

"Does he follow you?"

"Not so far. He just watches me come out of class. He sits in the truck, slumped down in the seat."

When Kirstin looked up, Fran saw fear. "If it is him, and you're not certain it is, he probably just wants to see if he's lost you to someone else."

Kirstin arose from the bed and walked to the window, her back to Fran. "He served time in prison. I never mentioned that little fact to my parents. I was afraid they would worry, and now I'm worried."

"Served time for what?" Fran wanted to know.

"He wouldn't say."

"Perhaps you should report this to the police."

"I want to be sure. I feel bad about breaking up with him, because it had to do with me more than him, and I don't want to get him in trouble if he hasn't done anything."

"I'm glad you told me," Fran said. "Let me know if it happens again, and try to get the license number. What's that banging noise?"

"The workman. I hope they finish soon."

"When do your parents get home?"

"Friday."

Fran said, "I better go home or my kids will think I've taken a cruise."

On the way out, they passed a TV. Fran heard a name she recognized. "Are you hurt? Have you been in an accident? Call Arthur Fishburn."

She paused. "That's him. That man is suing my paper."

There was Fishburn, standing in front of a crudely painted backdrop of what was evidently intended to suggest a pier. He wore plaid shorts, a Hawaiian print shirt, black socks and running shoes. He held a fishing pole. Smiling broadly, he cast the line with exaggerated effort, a gold chain around his neck emerging from the "V" in his shirt. A voiceover intoned, "In a bind? Call the Fish." Fishburn jerked wildly, an imagined catch about to pull him overboard. He planted his feet and began to reel in. The pole did not bend because hooked to the other end was a large, green cardboard sign spangled with "$$$$$". Fishburn held up his catch as the voiceover broke into a jingle: "Car wreck? Train wreck? Airplane crash? Slip and fall we do it all, call Arthur Fishburn."

Fran shook her head in disbelief.

111

Kirstin said, "You're lucky you don't have a TV. Those run all day."

"How dreadful," Fran said.

Chapter 41

New I Takes Shape, and that Shape is Doughnut

Over the next several months, Art acquired options on an impressive 225,000 additional acres. Overshadowing this substantial achievement was the fact that the ultimate tract, all 325,000 acres, was contiguous, meaning that entry at any point allowed a future New Israeli to visit every square centimeter of New I without leaving its boundary. True, in some places this contiguousness was as narrow as twelve feet, but even that was wide enough for a railroad track. In shape, the amalgamated acreage resembled Manhattan as seen from the space shuttle, with enough widths, narrows, bends and angles to have been laid out by a legislative redistricting committee.

The single blight on the map of New I was the 10,000 acre parcel located more or less in the center, like Central Park. This parcel had proved thus far impossible to option because land records disclosed it was still owned by the Porkrind Trust, and tracking down anyone associated with the Trust had frustrated Art to tears. He had driven to Austin, to the address where, according to Tricksy, the tax bills went. The receptionist at the suite of rental offices told him that no one from Porkrind had been in for over a year and that their instructions were to forward all mail to a post office box in El Paso. Neither the receptionist nor any of the tenants seemed to know anyone employed by Porkrind. Because it was a legal trust organized under Texas law, Porkrind was required to have a registered agent, one P. R. O'Kelly of the Dallas law firm of Hoover, Coolidge and Harding. Art tried him next, but O'Kelly hinted at an unpaid invoice and said in any event he was bound by attorney-client privilege to reveal no further information. O'Kelly would only commit to an effort to contact his client, taking Art's phone number.

Art duly reported to OYEVEY the difficulties he was encountering in putting into place the "last crumb of the cake," by which he meant the last piece of the pie. He expressed complete confidence that securing Porkrind's option was a foregone conclusion in view of the minimal uses to which landlocked acreage could be put. OYEVEY's executive committee gave its unanimous approval (the first unanimous vote on record) to authorize Art to exercise the options he had collected, subject only to his securing the last option for the Porkrind tract. At an average price of $3,500 an acre, the committee spent most of its time and energy raising the $1.2 billion required to exercise its options and close the deal. It also hired Tel Aviv architects sworn to the utmost secrecy, so that construction of the capitol could begin shortly after deed recordation.

Art, having succeeded in 99% of his essential mission and believing he had secured for himself a niche in New I's pantheon of heroes, spent his time between Tricksy's house and various points of interest in Centerfield, a town essential to the future as the county seat of Bucko County. He had learned enough about Texas to anticipate a certain native resistance when it became known that a new sovereign and independent nation was to be established in the middle of their state. This untidy detail was not Art's responsibility, however, as OYEVEY had tapped others to calm these particular waters. Israel had powerful friends in the U.S., and once OYEVEY's ambassadors set to work explaining how much money the U.S. could save by writing off the Middle East after Israel's successful relocation, resistance would fade until it ultimately disappeared with time, say 500 or 1000 years.

One point of interest in Centerfield was the newspaper. Since his initial option payment, Art had disciplined himself to read the *Sentinel* from front to back, ads included. He found its editorial obsession with barbeque somewhat odd, but entertainingly so. The devoting of 12 pages to high school football seemed justified by the amount of interest surrounding it, but certainly nothing like it existed in Israel. For international news, there was always CNN or the Dallas newspapers, but for locum smokum, the *Sentinel* was tough to beat.

Chapter 42

Todd Works on his Moves

Following the meeting at SNEEZE, Todd Melville had taken Fran to dinner, where for the first time he made an overt gesture toward something more than friendship. They sat at a small, candle-lit table in the Limp Noodle, a pasta restaurant that had just opened in Centerfield. After a glass of wine, he reached across the table and seized her hand. She did not withdraw it.

"I like you very much," Melville said.

"I like you, too," Fran said.

"You've never talked about your husband."

Fran said, "You've never asked. I've appreciated that."

"Is it too early to ask now?"

"Not at all." Fran told him about Jim, about how they had met in high school and married too early, about how they had planned to wait for children and how that plan had gone amiss, and how they never regretted it. She told him that Jim had been the gentlest man she had ever known, and that when he came home he never failed to hug her, during which few seconds she felt sure nothing in the world could threaten her.

"And how about you?" she asked. "Tell me about Nan Tucker." Her hand felt clammy so she reached for her napkin to break his hold.

"An old story, I'm afraid. Boy meets girl, leaps before he really looks hard enough, and then spends the next few years regretting. Gradually, we drifted apart. I threw myself into my work while she threw herself at another man. But I don't harbor any grudges."

"That's very sad," Fran said.

"Oh, it was my fault as well." He sipped his wine. "I see now that she was lonely, feeling washed up at only thirty-five. I should have been more attentive. If the chance ever comes again, I will be."

Now it was Fran's turn to sip. "We all have a few regrets," she said vaguely.

In the unlighted parking lot after dinner, Todd kissed her. She let him. It felt both strange and familiar. Unconsciously, she waited for a feeling that nothing in the world could threaten her, but it didn't come.

Chapter 43

The Best Defense is an Offensive One

Rick Lopez did not look forward to telling Ed Abernathy that, upon further research, they had no chance of winning an abuse of process counter-suit against Fishburn. "The law," Rick explained, "permits suits that do not always seem well founded because it wants to protect access to the courts by ordinary citizens."

"In other words," Ed said, "Fishburn can sue me for Sagittarianism and I'm stuck defending it."

"What the hell is that?"

"The act of being a Sagittarian."

"Yes."

Ed reacted by throwing his putter at a plant in Rick's office.

Rick sought to console. "At least your insurance company is paying my fees. This won't run you out of business."

"We've got to do something," Ed insisted. "I'm not about to lie down in the middle of the road and let this bus driver and his caravan of fifty-thousand Tanyas run over me."

"Let's win the case. Then you can write editorials about the whole ordeal."

"Do we have to wait until we win?"

"It would be prudent," Rick said.

"Why?"

"You might give him grounds to add more damages to his lawsuit."

"What's he going to do, find more Tanyas? No, I've decided. We're going after him. I'll get Fran to re-run the Tanya-does-Wall-More piece. We'll show Fishburn we don't care how many people he claims to represent."

"It's your call," Rick said.

Ed returned to his office and handed down instructions. "It may cost me this newspaper and you your jobs, but we're going down swinging. We'll run this story every week if we have to."

The blatant defiance of danger by a tiny weekly like the *Sentinel* drew the attention of the more powerful newspapers in Texas, who sent reporters to Fishburn & Associates for comment. Fishburn himself appeared in his oak-paneled library to field questions. A Dallas morning paper wanted to know what he thought of the *Sentinel's* challenge.

"It will cost them dearly," Fishburn predicted. "Why, just today we've been contacted by over four hundred more Tanyas."

"How many does that make now?"

"At last count we have topped 55,000."

When the *Sentinel* again ran the story the following week, the media again descended on Fishburn's office. The count now exceeded 60,000, according to an associate who informed the curious that Mr. Fishburn was in depositions and therefore unavailable. Fishburn had authorized him to report, however, that due to the *Sentinel's* flagrant and insistent disregard for his clients, he would amend his lawsuit to seek punitive damages, bringing the total sought to $4.5 billion. This time, the story made the evening news. The *Sentinel's* circulation surged. Golfers praised Ed at every tee and green, urging him to keep up the fight. Ed developed a standard response to these well-meaning encouragements: "Don't worry about us," he said. "Sooner or later they'll run out of Tanyas, but we'll never run out of ink."

"I have more good news," Fran told Ed after recounting the most recent advertising revenues. "The Centerfield Town Council is going to consider establishing a child protective services unit. We may finally be getting through."

"Good work," said Ed, smiling. "I'm proud of us."

Chapter 44

Chip, a Slip and Some Lip

Chip found himself alone again with Ms. Heckmon. This time, on the pretext of stretching her metal detecting wand to his good hip, she pressed her ample breasts against his arm, letting them rest there until he turned away, blushing.

"I don't think you like me, Chip," she said.

Chip said nothing then, but he had plenty to say to Fran that evening. She listened, jotted down a couple of quotes on the back of an electric bill envelope, and appeared at the school the following morning. She asked to see Helen Irons, the principal, who was evidently in a meeting.

"Please interrupt her," Fran said.

"I'm afraid I can't do that," said a blasé secretary. "She's going over a new insurance plan with some of the teachers."

"I'll wait fifteen minutes," Fran said, seating herself in a waiting area outside Irons's office.

Minutes later, Irons arrived. She greeted Fran warily, leaning slightly back as she shook her hand, as though Fran's left hand held a snake. Her demeanor seemed to ask, "what now?," a question Fran sensed she asked often during an average day.

"We have a problem," Fran announced after Irons had closed the door to her office. She related Chip's experiences with Heckmon.

When she had finished, Irons said, "We certainly can't have that. I'll take her off the security detail."

"Is that it?"

"That will solve your son's problem, won't it?"

"Perhaps," Fran said, "but aren't other students at risk?"

"We've had no other complaints."

"Maybe others haven't come forward."

Irons stared at the ceiling, as if to contemplate such a possibility.

119

Fran said, "I'm getting the feeling you don't believe me."
"Well . . ."
"Well what?"
Irons shifted in her chair. "It's just that Ms. Heckmon is an avowed lesbian."
"I've spotted a small problem," Fran said. "Evidently, she likes boys."
Irons giggled. "Now that would be a problem," she said. "Oh, I wish we could get rid of these metal detectors. Who am I going to get to staff that thing?"
"I'm sure you'll figure something out. In the meantime, I think you need to investigate Ms. Heckmon and her relationship with other students. There is a more serious problem than staffing the metal detector."
Ms. Irons winced. "That won't be easy."
"Why not?"
"The school board will have a fit. It took them several years to recruit an Eskimo, and depending on the outcome of the investigation we may have to get rid of her."
"Ms. Heckmon is an Eskimo?"
"Of Eskimo descent, yes. I think it was her grandmother on her father's side—I'd have to check her personnel file. We have these recruitment goals, and it's not easy to recruit Eskimos in Texas, I can tell you that."
Fran arose. "Eskimo or not, lesbian or not, you need to keep her away from my son, are we understood?"
"Oh, I quite agree," said Irons. "We can't put up with any foolishness."

Chapter 45

Warning to Reader: Pun Ahead

The controversy over New Hampshire's own Brock Rutledge casting the deciding vote at the barbeque cook-off grew as the winter wore on. Ed had written some of his finest editorials, reaffirming the paper's commitment to tomato-based sauces and urging tolerance and patience among Centerfielders. He took particular pride in his most pontifical effort:

Those who believe that the importance of barbeque lies in filling an empty belly miss the point. Barbeque is more, so much more, than a dead pig or steer on a spit. To trace its evolution is to trace the evolution of society itself. On the east coast, particularly eastern North Carolina, a corner of the cradle of our great country, fundamentalists hold fast to the view that vinegar and peppers and a little water are the only true ingredients of a sauce. They condemn, even today, deviations from that gospel. So I ask, where are their great cities? Where are the advanced medical and research facilities to compare with those in Texas? Where are the great sports franchises and giant stadiums? Coincidence? Don't make me laugh, or chortle, or even chuckle. Do you still doubt me? Then let me ask this: where was "The Lost Colony"? Bingo! Eastern North Carolina. Do I claim that the Colony was Lost solely due to its recipe for barbeque sauce? No, that is going too far, but who can escape the correlation? When, we may rightly ask, will those good folks living in the past bring themselves into the modern era? When will they look westward, to behold the progress made by those of us who have been willing to convert to

121

tomato and molasses? I predict a dire future for those who subject themselves to the domination of a vinegar-based fanatical fringe. Their cities will crumble, their crops will fail, their cell phone reception will suffer—all such ills and more will befall them simply because they could not rid themselves of the orthodox extremists. But there is hope. Even in a place like Georgia, hardly a beacon of enlightenment by Texas standards, they have advanced to mustard-based sauces, and my sources tell me that in tailgates from Athens to Savannah the more progressive Georgians have been experimenting with sauces of mass appeal, and who can say when such recipes might be unleashed upon the rest of us. My fellow Centerfielders, I do not believe a man like Brock Rutledge poses a serious threat to our competition or to our way of life. He is, by all accounts, a good and decent man. Yes, he is from New Hampshire, but not everyone can be from Texas, and we must accept that as a universal truth. He has lived in Oklahoma for many years, and his conversion to our philosophy is confirmed by this simple fact: in his award-winning recipe for barbeque sauce, there is not an ounce of vinegar. He has shared the recipe with me so that I could confirm what I am reporting to you. If a man will go so far as to share his barbeque secrets, you can trust him and take his word to the bank.

Notwithstanding Ed's appeal to reason, fissures in the Centerfield Body Politic deepened, forcing Ed to write yet another editorial. This time, he likened the controversy to Michael Jackson's death in a way that escaped Fran and other readers. Despite his efforts, 142 contestants threatened to boycott Bustamonte Day altogether unless another judge was found. Rutledge, who had considered resignation when the controversy first arose, now dug in, stating on the record that his fairness and impartiality, indeed the fairness and impartiality of all New Hampshireites, hung in the balance. He vowed to fight any effort to un-invite him.

The mayor, who had so effectively diffused the only previous political crisis in Centerfield's history, the naming of the town itself, planned to retire in Florida at the end of his term. Attention he would normally have focused on the Brock Rutledge issue suffocated under reams of brochures about gated enclaves with "vibrant" homeowners associations and no yard maintenance.

Election of the mayor's successor offered another potential crisis. Some had suggested that the great Buster should declare himself a candidate. As he currently divided his time between baseball card shows, where he signed autographs for $10 each, and hunting and fishing trips to exotic sites, Buster possessed both the time and the prestige for the job. No one doubted that the great Buster could, if he declared himself a candidate, avert the crisis that threatened to sully the award named for him, the Bustamonte Barbeque Prize, and absolutely no one doubted he would be elected should he choose to run.

Except Fran.

"Why don't you run for mayor?" she asked Todd Melville over dinner. They were eating seafood.

"For starters, the rumor is that Buster is going to run. I have it on good authority that a delegation of ten, including the current mayor and your own Ed Abernathy, approached him with the idea, and he promised to consider it."

"That may be," said Fran, who knew very well that the rumor was true, "but that doesn't mean he's qualified to be mayor."

"He's in the Baseball Hall of Fame; that seems to qualify him to a lot of people around here."

Fran knew this to be true as well. She had argued the point with Ed prior to his visit with the delegation. "Just because the town is named after him doesn't mean he should be mayor," she had said. "Churchill saved England and the British turned him out in the next election," to which Ed had replied, "They did?"

"Why don't you run?" Todd Melville asked her.

"That's all I need, and all the town needs, too. Besides, I like writing editorials. It's my niche."

"And you do it so well," Melville said.

"Cut the smooze," she said. "Okay, don't cut it entirely."

"I'm guessing you haven't been behind these diatribes on the Brock Rutledge barbeque issue."

"Those are Ed's," Fran said, smiling.

Todd Melville carefully partitioned off a bite of roasted salmon. As he lifted the fork to his mouth he said, "You get war, peace, and almost everything in between, and Ed does the heavy lifting on barbeque."

"We all have our strengths," she said. "At first I thought the entire flap over judging a barbeque contest was completely frivolous, but now I see a certain tension emerging that is good for us. After all, Brock Rutledge is a stranger, highly mistrusted just because he's from New Hampshire. Ed is merely urging tolerance; that's a good lesson for any town to learn."

"But all these dire warnings about tearing the town apart—"

"Don't you think it could?"

"Maybe. But I'd caution him about letting the paper become a tract that is constantly proselytizing over something like barbeque. I mean, Michael Jackson?"

"That was over the top, I'll admit. But I still don't see the danger."

"It's obvious," Melville said. "Don't you realize what could happen if the *Sentinel* becomes a warning tract in Centerfield?"

Fran suppressed a grin. "Someone could hit the wall?"

"So true."

Chapter 46

Too Obese to Run, George Nevertheless Darts

George Fafalone's excitement mounted as the Irish Pub entered the final stages of completion. On the day the dart board was installed, he insisted that Joyce, Kirstin and Scott join him for an inaugural game. The bar-length mirror, a special order item, had yet to be installed, and the bar stools, another special order item, had yet to arrive, but the ambiance of an Irish pub was undeniable once the Guinness keg had been tapped. Kirstin asked her father if he had any objection to inviting Fran over.

"None," he said. "Maybe she can throw darts."

Joyce, Scott, Kirstin and Fran stood in a semicircle. With a flourish George opened the sealed package of darts he had ordered over the internet weeks before in anticipation of this moment. He grasped one between his index finger and thumb, assaying its balance and heft. Satisfied, he let it fly toward the board. It struck the paneling below the target, firmly embedding. He smiled sheepishly, then said, "It may take a few to get my touch."

It took quite a few, but by the third or fourth game George became a force to be reckoned with as he found the bull's eye with moderate regularity. He walked ten feet from the toe line, retrieved his darts, and returned, soon working up a sweat visible at his hair line. After game six he passed, saying he needed a break. He poured himself a Guinness and sat out the next round. "Makes a man feel like he's sitting in Dublin," he said with satisfaction, panting faintly.

"You rest," cautioned Joyce. "You can't afford to over exert yourself."

Fran excused herself, saying she had to return home to supervise homework. George told her to return soon for a rematch, and Kirstin walked her to the door. Joyce asked Scott how things were going at the hospital.

"Okay," he said.

"You're still interested in becoming a doctor, right?" Joyce asked.

"I never said I would become a doctor," he replied, tossing his next dart with added zest. He and Kirstin seesawed in a close match.

Joyce brightened. "George, you know what we need in here? A juke box."

"I don't think Irish pubs have juke boxes," George said.

"They must," she insisted.

"I've never heard of one with a juke box," he said.

"What do they do for entertainment?"

"They talk," Scott said. "And play darts."

"Well, they can't possibly sit there all evening and talk," Joyce said.

Kirstin poised her dart, then said, "Mom, Irish pubs have been around for a long time. Before electricity. I think Dad's right." She threw, striking the bull's eye and turning smugly to Scott.

"What a shame," said Joyce. "Some music would be so nice with the whole family together like this."

George said, "Kirstin, I haven't seen what's-his-face around."

"You mean Pete?" Kirstin asked.

"Yeah, him. Harley man."

"You won't see him again. He's history."

"You broke up?" Joyce asked.

"I invited him to hit the highway like weeks ago," Kirstin replied over her shoulder as she retrieved her darts.

"How did he take it?" Joyce asked.

"He wasn't happy, but I was, so that's that."

Joyce paused before saying, "He's not a bunny boiler, is he?"

"What's a bunny boiler?" George demanded.

"You remember," the voice of Joyce said. "*Fatal Attraction*. Glenn Close boiled Michael Douglas's daughter's bunny because he broke up with her."

George sighed as Kirstin said, "I don't think so."

Scott said, "We don't have a bunny."

"I've got it," said Joyce, "I'll put a juke box in the Solarium."

126

Chapter 47

Fran Loses One, Wins Two

On the following morning Fran received a letter from the Big Toe HMO, regretting to inform her that after due deliberation, with "faithful consciousness to the health of our members," her request for Sarah's throat culture remained denied. But, "because we put people first at Big Toe HMO," this adverse decision could be appealed to a medical panel consisting of one doctor, one nurse, and one consumer ombudsman. She tossed it in the garbage with the remains of a tuna fish sandwich. Then, she dressed for work. As she was walking out her door, the phone rang.

"Fran, it's Ed."

"Hello, Ed. I'm on my way."

"That's why I'm calling. The AC's out here. Hot as hell in the office. I suggest you work at home this morning. The repair people are on the way. I'll call you when they get it fixed."

"Toss me in the briar patch," she said. She replaced her shoes with slippers and sat down at her home computer. At three, Chip arrived from school.

"Ms. Heckmon won't come near me," he reported. "Whatever you said to Mrs. Irons did the trick."

"Good. How do the female students get along with her?"

"Okay, I guess. Why?"

"Just curious. Has she ever mentioned being part Eskimo?"

"Not to me."

The phone rang. Ed gave the all clear. Fran exchanged her slippers for shoes and left. When she opened the door to the *Sentinel's* office, she saw balloons just as the staff screamed out "Congratulations!" Ed, front and center, stood beaming, a plaque in his hand.

"What's going on?" she asked amidst backslaps.

Ed cleared his throat, signaling quiet. "The Texas Press Association announced its annual prizes last night. First place for editorials went to us. Since the paper has never before been recognized for anything beyond its support of the United Way, this is a milestone in our history. You've competed with the best and brought home the bacon." Applause broke out.

Fran stammered, "Who . . . how?"

"I took the liberty of submitting some of your best pieces." Ed said. "And our war against Fishburn didn't hurt. They called me this morning to let me know we'd won. There is an awards ceremony in Dallas next month. I want you to accept for the *Sentinel*."

Ed invited everyone back into his office, where champagne and finger food awaited. As she sipped champagne and took compliments from her co-workers, Fran reflected on the remarkable year this had become. She had never envisioned herself as an award winning editorialist, but rather as a classifieds clerk grubbing for a check twice a month. Then again, until three years before she had pictured her life as a wife and mother, and fifty percent of that equation had died with Jim. How unpredictable life can prove, she marveled, and she wasn't sure whether to be comforted by the thought or terrorized by it. One day, and we never know what day, she told herself, all will be predictable and certain. Until that day, and the eternity which follows it, "I will be comforted by change, in all its forms," she resolved. "The absence of change is the only true terror."

The work day ended and the staff disbursed, leaving Fran and Ed seated in his office. He raised his glass, sloshing some champagne on his pants. He reached into his desk drawer and drew out a folder. "I waited for the right time to give you this," he said. "And don't worry, the rest of the staff is going to be covered too."

Real health insurance, Fran saw as she perused its contents. Not in Albuquerque but right around the corner. "Thanks," she said. "This is huge."

"First prize for editorials is also huge," Ed said. "I wish my pappy had lived to see it."

Chapter 48

The Political Situation Clouds Up

On a Friday, Buster announced his candidacy for mayor, to great applause by many but to the disappointment of those who thought it impolitic that the news came from a spokesman rather than from the great man himself. When asked, the spokesman explained that Buster had been committed to an antique baseball card show for several weeks and did not want to sadden the young men and women who sought his autograph at such affairs. The same spokesman appeared flustered when it was observed that Buster controlled timing of the announcement, and thus had it within his power to avoid the scheduling conflict. When pressed for Buster's plans once elected, the spokesman said that Buster intended to assist a ghost writer who had been hired to pen his biography.

"That's not really what I meant," said the inquiring reporter from Houston. "What is his plan for the town?"

The spokesman cited his principal's heavy schedule of baseball card shows and stated that Buster had yet to focus on issues. He remained confident, however, that some statement regarding issues would be forthcoming, "possibly by election day."

Fran wasn't sure she wanted Todd Melville as her mayor, but she had concluded that some alternative to Buster had to be found. She did not dislike Buster, or baseball, but she thought the demands on the town's chief executive exceeded those Buster would be willing to shoulder. She appreciated the consensus that his candidacy would bring, at least until some decisions were required, but lack of controversy did not equate to peace or good government in her view. She conceded that a run against him bordered on the politically suicidal, but membership in the Baseball Hall of Fame should not convey the added benefit of unopposed election to high office. She decided to feel Melville out on the subject.

129

On a pleasant spring afternoon they sat on a picnic blanket in the park. "You owe it to yourself and the town to consider it," she told him.

"I'm flattered, Fran, really flattered," he said. "And I'd be lying if I denied any interest. My work at SNEEZE has given me renewed respect for public policy, and if I feel strongly I should be willing to pony up. The money wouldn't be a problem, but there are other problems. I have virtually no chance of winning, for openers."

"The odds are long," Fran admitted. She arranged a slice of salmon on a cracker and topped it with capers, handing it to Melville. "But with a better-than-expected showing, you might springboard yourself into another office. Congress, for example."

"There's another problem, as if getting beat wasn't enough. I'm not sure I'm eligible to run. My primary residence is in Dallas; I rent an apartment in Centerfield. There must be some requirement that the mayor reside here."

Fran looked skyward, where a puffy white cloud in the shape of a whale hung lazily overhead. "I hadn't given that a thought. I'll find out."

Chapter 49

Help a Brother Out

Scott swore Kirstin to secrecy before divulging his plan to meet 1sicksize9. He brought her into his confidence because he needed her help in covering his anticipated absence from home for one week.

"That's the dumbest idea I've ever heard," she said. "It could be anyone, a serial rapist for all you know. He's sick--he even admits it in his name. 1sicksize9, Scott. Hello!"

"I'm sure he's okay," he said. "We relate."

"You see? You know nothing about him."

"I know enough," Scott said. He wished to avoid a discussion of details, for he had few where his e-pal was concerned. His curiosity had inspired a methodical campaign, now months old, to learn some basic biographical information, but 1sicksize9 had shown himself to be both reticent and guarded where his private life was concerned.

"Such as?"

"Such as he lives in Mobile, Alabama."

"And how do you know that?"

"Because I send checks there and I get photographs back, if you have to know."

"You have an address?"

"Of course." In truth, he had only a post office box number.

"Well, at least that's something," Kirstin said. "Scott, listen to me. People in prison have access to the internet. Child molesters use the internet. Murderers use the internet. You can't just charge off to meet someone like that. Will you get some counseling? You can borrow my shrink. Please don't meet this weirdo."

Scott could see she meant well, and he also foresaw that she was concerned enough to tell George and Joyce should he persist. "Maybe you're right," he said.

131

Chapter 50

Culture Clashes

On the day after Scott persuaded Kirstin that she had persuaded him not to meet 1sicksize9, a car bomb exploded in Jerusalem, killing five people. Within hours, Israeli planes attacked a Palestinian police headquarters, killing three. Fran approached Ed about writing an editorial on the escalating violence in the Middle East, but Ed expressed little enthusiasm. He reminded her that the controversy over Brock Rutledge's participation as a judge in the barbeque cook-off was of greater interest to their readership, and for the *Sentinel* to stray too far from its readership was risky, particularly in view of Ed's recent ruminations about making the paper a daily.

"Exactly why we need to broaden our vision," Fran insisted.

"Leave it alone," Ed countered. His real concern was not the dilution of the paper's focus on local issues but rather the pesky questions he might get at the golf course. If the *Sentinel* took positions on matters in Europe or the Middle East, someone could press him for details, like what exactly that Bank was West of. As he confided to his buddy Sam after several drinks, "I don't know the West Bank from the Sperm Bank." They had enjoyed a brief chuckle over that one.

Ed penned his final editorial on the Brock Rutledge brouhaha by telling his readers to respect the decision of the judges as final and legitimate. He reminded them that it was entirely possible, even likely, that the winning entry would receive unanimous support from the judges ("all the truly great recipes do," he wrote) and that in such an event the opinion of a judge born in New Hampshire could not be outcome determinative. It was only, he reasoned, when the two Texas judges disagreed that Rutledge's opinion actually mattered, and on the virtues of barbeque the town could have every expectation that Texans would know a winner when they gnawed down on it. Ed could remember few editorials that provided him with deeper satisfaction, and the compliments extended around tees and greens convinced him he had hit just the right tone.

Fran's interest in writing an editorial on the Middle East persisted, but when she sat down to do it she saw that in one respect Ed's advice had been sound; she simply didn't know enough about the subject to meaningfully opine on it. She began to study the history of that tortured region, of hostilities as old as time, of attacks and counterattacks so pervasive and repetitious that everyone could claim retaliation and no one could dispute it, of competing claims for statehood and for ultimate control of a square mile of conflict called Jerusalem. "What a mess," she said to herself. "I'm glad it's on the other side of the world."

After an afternoon spent at the public library, with her mind numbed by re-drawn boundary and occupation lines, she returned home to a message that the Big Toe HMO had called. She placed what she anticipated to be her last long distance call to Albuquerque.

"Rosetta Aldama, please."

"Rosetta is no longer with us. This is Carman Mesones, may I help you?"

"I should have notified you," Fran said. "I have other insurance now. Please tell Dr. Punjabi to close our files."

"We'll be sorry to lose you as a member of the Big Toe family."

"It's been . . . an experience," Fran said. "By the way, my son said someone called."

"Yes, that was me. I wanted to tell you that the review committee has turned down your request for the throat culture, but Dr. Punjabi advises you to appeal because the vote was two to one and he believes the senior review committee is even more committed to patient health than this lower level committee."

Fran laughed. "I needed that culture months ago. Please thank the committee for me, but they can move on to more important matters."

"Nothing is more important than our patients."

"But I am no longer one of those. Have a great day."

133

Chapter 51

Kirstin Puts Puberty Behind Her

As Kirstin had never visited the offices of the *Sentinel* before, Fran did a double-take when she thought she saw her come in. Fran left her office to greet her.

"You look troubled," Fran said.

"I'm a little down," Kirstin said. "It's nothing and it's everything. I hope I'm not interrupting you."

Fran led her through cubicles, introduced her to several staff members, and closed the door when they arrived back at Fran's office.

"Tell me about it," Fran said, offering her a chair. "I have time."

"Here's the license plate number. You told me to get it. It's a blue truck, a Ford I think." She handed Fran a slip of paper.

"So Pete won't give up."

"What a creep, and to think I actually slept with him."

"Don't beat yourself up," Fran counseled. "The fact that you no longer buy his act is a very good sign. It means your self-image is rising."

"I guess. Turning my life around is . . . "

"Hard?"

"That's the word."

"Come in," Fran said in response to a knock at the door.

A petite young woman with reddish hair entered the office, handed Fran a sheet of paper, and smiled at Kirstin as Fran read and initialed it. "Sorry to interrupt," she said.

"That was Jane," Fran said when the young woman left. "She's divorced with two kids and no child support."

"In other words, stop feeling sorry for myself," Kirstin said.

Fran shook her head. "I didn't mean that at all. You've come a long way, Kirstin. A little self pity won't hurt."

"You know what I've learned?"

134

"I'm betting quite a bit."

"I've learned that I didn't see very much of what was going on around me. I don't know how I missed this stuff but I did. Remember the day you laid into me? When you said my dad was a loser and Mom was a ditz? It's so true. How can I have missed something so basic? It's like I've been in this serious fog."

"You're just maturing, that's all. I was pretty brutal on George and Joyce because I wanted to shock you into opening your eyes. Now that you've done that, you'll find they also have some good qualities."

"Such as?"

"They're together. Staying married isn't easy."

Kirstin seemed to ponder this as she stared out the window. A silence ensued. Then she said, "I sit there in these classes and I think of how much time I wasted and I want to cry."

"Do it, but then start studying again."

"Was I asleep in high school?"

"No, you were self-absorbed, as so many people are. Here's a little experiment you can run. The next time you're eating lunch, listen to the conversation at the table next to you. If it's like most of the ones I hear, one person will tell the other some fact or story about himself or herself, and the other person will listen without asking any questions or making any thoughtful comment. That's because the second person in this so-called conversation is not really paying any attention to what's being said; the second person is merely waiting for the first to finish so he or she can relate their own fact or story, which will in turn produce no questions or meaningful comment from person number one, and on and on it goes until lunch is finished, and if you listen closely enough you realize that each of these people has been talking to himself about himself. What you have are two self-absorbed people focused on their own needs and interests to the exclusion of others, and I'm afraid it's an epidemic out there. That's one reason I like working for a newspaper. It forces me to take an interest in what's going on outside my own little world. Reading a newspaper will do the same thing, by the way. There's a lot going on in the world, and when something big happens, even something bad, it reminds us all that

135

we're in this together and it forces us to concentrate on others. Well, enough of my sermonizing."

Another silence ensued. "What's that?" asked Kirstin, pointing to a plaque on the wall.

"I lucked out. The paper won an award."

"Cool," Kirstin said, rising to read the inscription. "Maybe I'll apply for a job here."

"Maybe you should. Can you write?"

Chapter 52

Enough to Make a Grown Lawyer Weep

The class action known as *Fifty-thousand Tanyas v. Wall-More et al.* entered what lawyers call the "discovery phase," in theory a process intended to present each side with the opportunity to learn enough about the other's case to prevent surprise at trial, but in practice a means by which lawyers, expert witnesses and court reporters bill and collect tens of thousands of dollars in fees. As Fishburn often said while chuckling in that peculiar way of his, accompanied by wafts of purplish vapors from his last meal, "Discovery is like having your client's ATM card with no daily withdrawal limit."

Fishburn did less chuckling in this particular case because the Tanyas he represented, now over sixty-thousand strong, had no money to pay for discovery, a situation not unprecedented in class actions. That required Fishburn & Associates to advance the costs of experts and court reporters, with the result that Fishburn now confronted the unpleasant reality that his firm stood in a hole some half-million dollars deep, with no assurance it would eventually recover these costs, not to mention legal fees. He took solace in knowing that the value of publicity being generated by his war with the *Sentinel*, now reported by newspapers all over Texas and beyond, vastly exceeded any sum he might be risking in the litigation itself.

Rick Lopez looked across his conference table at the expert witness he was about to depose. Cases such as this one often came down to a battle of experts. To his right sat Ed Abernathy, representing the *Sentinel*, and to Ed's right sat a plump Wall-More greeter from the local store, emblematic of Wall-More's contempt for the lawsuit, which it considered frivolous. The court reporter swore Martha Hienz, Ph.D., a clinical psychologist currently treating eighteen Tanyas from the Houston area. She sat rigidly in her chair, her hair pulled back and her hands folded with academic precision in her lap. Fishburn, his game face on, sat beside her. The Wall-More greeter, wearing a badge identifying her as Lucille, waved and smiled as Dr. Heinz took her oath. After some preliminary questions about her background and education, Lopez got down to the business.

"Dr. Heinz, I show you now what has been marked as plaintiff's exhibit No. 5,141, which appears to be a medical record for Tanya No. 5,141; do you recognize it?"

"Yes. Tanya No. 5,141 is my patient."

"When did you begin seeing her?" Lopez asked.

Dr. Heinz consulted the record before answering. "About four months ago."

"In other words," said Lopez, "about the time this lawsuit was filed?"

"That would be correct."

"Did she call to make the appointment or was it someone from Mr. Fishburn's office?"

"I object," said Fishburn.

"On what basis?" Lopez asked.

"Well . . . it's . . . irrelevant."

"Answer the question," Lopez instructed.

"I believe the appointment was scheduled by someone in Mr. Fishburn's office."

"What was your primary diagnosis?"

"Tanya No. 5,141 suffers from post traumatic stress disorder, or PTSD."

"And the trauma would be?"

"Her name appearing in the newspaper, accused of beating her son, Jerome, in Wall-More."

"So Tanya No. 5,141 reads the *Sentinel*?"

"A neighbor mentioned having seen it, I believe. Tanya No. 5,141 felt humiliated."

"I see," said Lopez. "And can you describe the stress you claim she suffered."

"Is suffering," Heinz corrected. "Her recovery has a long way to go."

"Of course," Lopez said.

Heinz crossed her legs smartly as she made eye contact with Lopez. "She feels alienation from her friends and family, particularly Jerome, repressed by a society indifferent to her needs as a person. A heightened sense of vulnerability has produced a fear of leaving her house, flying on airplanes, and scuba diving. She has become a compulsive eater of chocolate chip cookie dough ice cream. This compulsion has, in turn, produced a dramatic weight gain, which is contributing to her depression. She reports marked periods of self-doubt and feelings of worthlessness. She has come to believe that a vast conspiracy is targeting her for elimination. She has recurring nightmares of pigeons carrying her away."

Lopez interrupted. "Pigeons?"

"She fears being dropped from a great height. It's quite common. She is unable to work and has considered harming herself in some way."

"She is suicidal?"

"She has shown some early warning signs, yes."

"And what is your prognosis?"

"She will need years of expensive—excuse me, extensive counseling, and she will need to remain on antidepressants indefinitely."

"And is it your opinion, to a reasonable degree of medical certainty, that all of this stems from a comment made by her neighbor about an article in the paper?"

"Absolutely. Direct correlation. She weeps a lot. I forgot that."

Lopez turned toward Ed and winked. "Dr. Heinz, are you being compensated for your testimony here today?"

"Of course."

"At what rate?"

"Five hundred dollars per hour."

Lopez picked up another chart and slid it across the highly polished conference table. "Doctor, let me show you what has been marked as plaintiff's exhibit No. 16,704. Isn't it true that your patient Tanya No. 16,704 has the same complaints as Tanya No. 5,141?"

"Not at all. Tanya No. 16,704 has no fear of scuba diving, nor does she care for chocolate chip cookie dough ice cream."

139

"And the pigeons?"

"Seagulls. All patients are unique."

Chapter 53

Scott Meets P.T. Barnum's Grandchild

Scott knew he took certain risks by seeking out 1sicksize9, but he thought he had devised a plan that would minimize that risk. With patience, he might be able to size up his e-pal from a safe distance. On the pretext of visiting a college, he bought an airplane ticket to Mobile.

"What college are you looking at?" Joyce asked.

"The University of Mobile," he said.

"I haven't heard of that one. Do they have a football team?"

"It's fairly new," he said. "They're strong in pre-med."

He flew out on a Thursday, having mailed a check to 1sicksize9's post office box two days before. On the plane he grew darkly pessimistic, sensing futility overlaid by awkwardness. Why did he need to meet? Was his fetish more than the casual diversion he had assumed? Would his pal misinterpret his motives or worse, see things he didn't and thereby arrive at conclusions that had thus far escaped Scott? Was he truly sick — sicker than 1sicksize9?

He landed, took a cab to the post office, and walked idly around in search of the best vantage point. His first surprise came when he realized that P.O. Box 16, the familiar address, was a larger commercial box. He had always envisioned it as small, the smallest rental available, and tucked into a dimly lit corner.

The post office hummed with a steady stream of counter customers and box checkers. From a spot not visible to postal employees staffing the counter, his view of Box 16 was distant but unimpeded. From his jacket he took a stack of blank envelopes, lined them up in stacks, and appeared to be addressing them at glacial speed. After twenty minutes, he picked them up, walked around inside, went outside for a few minutes, then returned to his vantage point.

His apprehension returned. What if he was now under observation by a security camera or two way mirror? What if three unseen FBI agents were about to emerge from behind the package counter? He left, breathed some fresh air to calm himself, then returned with the self-assurance that he risked paranoia. It grew late. Fifteen minutes before closing he left, confident that his man was a morning person and could thus be expected early the following day. He found a modest motel room near the river, ordered a pizza to be delivered, and went to bed.

The following day he resumed his stakeout. At mid-morning he began to notice a postal employee who seemed to be making frequent trips through the area of Scott's observation counter. He thinks I'm going to go postal, Scott told himself. He considered running away, and might have done so had he not, at that moment, noticed someone approach the area of P.O. Box 16. He watched as the visitor bent slightly at the waist, dialed the combination, and removed from Box 16 a large stack of envelopes and papers. As she turned, Scott saw full-face a woman of about eighty, white hair, hunched noticeably and holding the mail with withered hands. She wore dark blue sweat pants, running shoes, and a tee shirt emblazoned with a Rolling Stones tour schedule.

"Christ," muttered Scott. "His mother or grandmother must pick up his mail. I didn't think of that."

The woman paused at a counter and rested her pile on its surface. As she began to sort the envelopes from the magazines and bulk items, Scott resolved to approach her, rationalizing that he would not want to follow her even if he could. He would simply ask her to introduce him to 1sicksize9. He approached, tapped lightly on the counter near the two piles of sorted mail, and waited.

"Yes?" the woman said, looking up. Her left ear was pierced and from it hung a silver pendant Scott had not previously observed.

"Excuse me. I'm looking for a friend. He rents this box, I think."

The woman stared at him, an envelope in one hand poised over the smaller pile. "What's the name?" she asked.

Scott did not immediately reply. Finally, he said meekly, "His name?"

"Your friend's name. He has a name, yes? If not, you'll have a tough time finding him."

142

Scott saw this as funny in a nervous, uncomfortable way. "Of course he does, but I know him by a street name, I guess you'd call it. Would you mind telling me who rents the box?"

"I do," she said. "Who are you?"

"My name's Scott. From Texas."

"Scott from Centerfield, Texas?"

"That's right."

The woman extended her hand. "Nice to meet you, Scott. I'm Emily Tabor." She smiled for the first time, a wide-denture grin.

"Does anyone else get their mail here?"

"Just me."

"I've been sending checks . . ."

"And I've been cashing them. It's not often I get to meet one of my on-line partners."

Scott stiffened. "You mean you're 1sicksize9?"

"Yep. Surprised?"

"Isn't that fraud or something?

"Not at all. See these?" She came partially around the counter, lifting one foot in his direction. "Size 9."

"But—"

"I'm sick, too. High blood pressure, osteoporosis—you will be too when you get to be my age. You have any idea what a month's supply of some of these prescription drugs cost these days? Of course you don't." She gathered up her mail. "Come outside. You look like you could use some air. We'll sit on the bench there and talk."

Scott did as he was told. Emily explained her need for medication and the money to pay for it, and how she was unable to work outside her small apartment. "Who would hire me?" she asked. She had discovered the internet five years before while visiting a grandchild. She realized almost immediately that the ability to remain anonymous opened up business opportunities.

As Scott listened, a form of depressed panic came over him. "I really am weird," he muttered.

She patted his knee. "You're not alone, if that's what you're worried about. I'll give you some contacts before you leave. I haven't done it up to now because I wanted to keep you as a customer. I wouldn't worry too much if I were you. Your fetish is harmless, unlike some others I could mention."

"You have other names?"

"About twenty. '2youngtodoit,' '1eagerlezzie,' '3beats2anytime' to name a few. I really hope none of them show up at the P.O."

Chapter 54

Fran Gets Carried Very Far Away, and Back

Fran's research confirmed that Todd Melville's lack of a permanent residence in Centerfield did not preclude his election as mayor. Her intuition echoed his—there must be some residency requirement, but no one, including Rick Lopez, could locate one in the town's charter or in any ordinance that had been passed. She resolved to write an editorial about the need for it.

Fran and Todd discussed the mayor's race over dinner. Abruptly, he placed his fork deliberately onto his plate and said, "Fran, don't you think it's time we slept together?"

"If you intend to run for mayor, you'll need to learn to be more evasive."

He folded his napkin, unfolded it, then spread it again on his lap. "I'm serious. We've been dating for some time. It's natural."

"I know about consummating a marriage, but a friendship?"

"You're playing with me now," he protested.

Fran saw that he would not be easily deflected. "That's sweet. Let me think about it."

"Haven't you? It's been months. I mean, if you're worried about . . . issues—"

"What issues?"

"You know."

"Maybe I don't. What issues?"

He cleared his throat. "Well, birth control, what if there's an accident, frozen embryos, surrogate parenting, AIDS; those issues."

"You left out global warming."

"You're hurting my feelings," he said, and she could tell that she had.

"Todd, let me explain something. You're a very nice man, and I consider you a good friend, but I don't sleep with someone because I enjoy dinner."

"What would it take?"

145

She paused, looked away momentarily, then said, "It would take holding my hand—"

"I've done that."

"You didn't let me finish. Holding my hand, then a kiss that gets extended, with an inquiring tongue that begins to probe and suggests to me another probe, lower down." She glanced at him as his breathing seemed to contract. Then she lowered her gaze as if to study her food. "I want to feel warmth in my hips and groin that makes them reach out for something reaching back. I want to press against his swelling and I want all of this pressing with my clothes on. Then, I want to feel his hands on my breasts, rubbing and teasing. I want to take my blouse off before he can, slip out of my bra while he watches, and guide his hands back to those breasts. I want him to fall to his knees while he unbuttons my skirt. After we finish, I want to curl up and listen for my babies at the other end of the hall and I want to fall asleep in the arms of their father who loves me and loves them and I want to wake up knowing that we will all be together and safe forever."

Fran's tears fell into her plate. "I'm so sorry," she said, her head still down. "That was the worst thing I've ever done in my life, and so totally unfair to you." She brought her napkin to her face and sobbed into it. When she finally looked up, Todd was gone.

Chapter 55

A Full Moon Rises as Fishburn's Sun Sets

Judge Gordon L. Frank peered over the rim of his half-moon glasses at Arthur Fishburn. In his hand, Judge Frank held Fishburn's brief opposing Wall-More's and the *Sentinel's* joint motion to deny class action status to Fishburn's complaint or, in the alternative, dismiss the case altogether. If granted, the first motion would require Fishburn to try each case separately, Tanya-by-Tanya, rather than all at once. One of Judge Frank's law clerks had done the math: Fishburn would be at least 381 years old by the time the jury returned the last verdict. By the time appeals were exhausted, the sun would have cooled measurably.

Gordon Frank sat on the bench he had occupied for nine years, having been elevated to his current duties and position after a bout of bizarre behavior during the weeks preceding his nomination. A closet alcoholic for years, he was widely admired for his skill as a trial lawyer, and he managed sobriety during the working day until his wife died, after which he lost his moorings. He began appearing at his office drunk, insulted clients, and behaved erratically. The crisis came when a long-time client gave him a bad check for work already performed. Frank learned that the client, a businessman, was closing a deal over breakfast at a local waffle house. He spotted them sitting in a booth by a large plate glass window. He approached the window, quite drunk, and turning his back, he lowered his pants and pressed his bare posterior to the glass in the approximate location of the salt, pepper and plastic menus. A former law partner interceded to prevent his arrest. The local bar association, mindful of his talents when sober, decided he needed the challenge of a judgeship. It worked. His last drink had been nine years ago, although the moniker of "Judge Moon" had been harder to shake.

"Mr. Fishburn, the court is troubled by this complaint. Assuming you prevail on this somewhat novel theory of liability, a

147

doubtful proposition at best, I fail to see how we can try all these cases together. Each of your clients must have reacted differently to the alleged defamation and conspiracy, meaning all of their damages are bound to be highly individualized. They lack what we call 'commonality.' Would you address that issue?"

Fishburn glanced over at Rick Lopez, who stared innocently into space. Ed Abernathy, seated beside Lopez, locked and unlocked two paper clips he fingered nervously. Beside Ed, Lucille, the Wall-More representative, smiled and waved at Fishburn for the eighth or ninth time.

"Your honor, would you please instruct this woman to stop harassing me. It's very distracting, and it's deliberate."

"Mr. Fishburn, are you referring to Lucille?"

"The same."

"She has a right to be here. She's representing a party defendant."

"Does she have to wave?"

"Evidently, she does. Proceed, Mr. Fishburn. I'm quite certain Wall-More thinks you have done your share of harassing in this matter."

Fishburn, flushed, cleared his throat. "The experts will testify that all of these Tanyas suffered PTSD, and while the subtleties of their experiences may vary in kind or degree, the essential impact is the same. Therefore, commonality is satisfied."

"Mr. Lopez, your response?" said Judge Frank.

"Judge, as we say here in Texas, Mr. Fishburn is all hat and no cattle. To bolster the alleged damages of his assembly line clients, he scheduled them all for cookie cutter mental evaluations by doctors who bought their degrees in flea markets on off-shore islands while on vacation. The evidence will show that all this manufactured fear and neurosis is imaginary. Pigeons. Seagulls. It's absurd."

Judge Frank nodded. "Mr. Fishburn, I am greatly troubled by this case. I'm going to take this motion under advisement, but if I were you I'd make every effort to settle this case before I rule.

"Your honor, she's waving again."

"Settlement, Mr. Fishburn. I recommend it."

Chapter 56

Fran Learns What Jeff is Not Allowed to Tell Her

Through a contact at the police department, Fran learned that Pete had done time for the crime of maiming, an aggravated assault that scars or disfigures the victim. Worried now, she pressed for more details. According to her source, Pete faced four additional years in prison if he should violate parole. His parole officer, one Jeff Hanson, lived in Houston.

Fran went to see Hanson, who worked out of a cubicle small enough to allow him to touch both side walls simultaneously when he extended his arms. He had played wide receiver at the University of Texas.

"You look like you could suit up tomorrow," Fran observed.

"Wouldn't I love it," he said. "Best days ever. I stay in shape."

Did he ever, Fran thought. She sat in the one chair Hanson's confined space would accommodate, transfixed by his combination of blue-black hair, cold blue eyes, a nose broken with just enough severity to be sexy, and long athletic limbs.

"Ever think about turning pro?"

"I thought about it, but none of the pro teams thought about it. The Caucasian affliction: good hands, slow feet."

"Too bad," Fran said. "How much can you tell me about one of your parolees?" She put the question casually, anticipating the precise answer she got.

"Nothing without his consent," Jeff said. "Sorry. I'd like to help, and I'm sure you wouldn't be here unless there was some problem. Is there?"

"Who's interviewing whom?" Fran asked half-heartedly, sensing that Jeff had her number.

There ensued the Hypothetical Game, forced upon them by Fran's need to protect Kirstin and Jeff's need to learn what he could about one of his parolees poised, he sensed, to break bad.

149

"Hypothetically," she said, "suppose one of your clients began stalking a young woman with whom he had been involved. Let's call her 'Kirstin' and your client . . . 'Pete.' What could you do?"

"Does this Pete have, hypothetically, time hanging over his head from a prior conviction?"

Fran nodded. "Let's say, hypothetically, he does. Several years."

"I see," said Jeff. "Then hypothetically I could revoke his parole because stalking is a crime, a violation of parole, and I don't have to wait for . . . Pete . . . to be convicted."

"Then all you'd need is a complaint from someone like Kirstin?"

"Hypothetically, yes, but there is more to it. It may help you to know that I think the prison system in this state — in the entire country for that matter — is a mess. In too many cases it turns abused, maladjusted kids into bisexual career criminals."

"So what's the answer? Leave them on the street?"

"No. I don't have the answer. I know the problems I see most start in the home, when these guys are infants. Even before they're infants if the mother is a druggie or a boozer. We take a boy who was born to an addicted mother, grew up with learning disabilities, raped or beaten, or both, by a succession of boyfriends or stepfathers, and then put him away when he doesn't turn out like you or me. It's nuts. I don't know who 'Pete' is, but if he's one of those, it will take more than a complaint for me to revoke his parole and put him back into that system." His blue eyes flashed, and Fran imagined thunder in the distance.

"Are you married?" Fran asked.

Jeff laughed. "Hypothetically?"

Fran laughed also. "No, really. You can tell me that, can't you?"

"I could, yes. Should I?"

"You should."

"In that case, no, I'm not married. Or engaged. My college love dumped me for a doctor. Why?"

"Just curious. The reporter's affliction."

150

Chapter 57

Todd is Revealed as Fran is Recruited

On the Saturday morning prior to Bustamonte Day, Fran brought Sarah and Chip with her to work at the *Sentinel*. As her work habits included a tendency to organize by a series of small piles, what she called her "piling cabinet," she barred the cleaning staff from her office, meaning she occasionally dusted and vacuumed it herself. In Ed's office, Sarah and Chip played the video games that Fran permitted on weekends. Ed found them there when he arrived just before noon.

"What are you doing here?" Fran asked when he passed by her door. She had finished cleaning and was in the process of reducing some of the piles she had just moved to dust. "It's Saturday."

"It is? I thought traffic seemed light."

She could not tell whether he was joking.

He entered her office, slouched into a chair, and propped his boots on her desk. "I've had an offer to buy the paper," he said. "A real sweet offer, at that."

Fran absorbed the news with outward calm. "What would you do?"

"That's just it," he said. "I really don't need the money. I need a purpose other than golf, don't you think?"

"Most people under seventy do."

"Besides, it's one of those huge media conglomerates--my pappy would roll over in his casket if I sold out to those bloodsuckers."

"Sounds like you're talking yourself out of selling."

"Maybe. But it's a ton of dough they're offering. I never imagined that a little old rag like the *Sentinel* could be worth that much." He raised his legs, crossed them at the ankles, and brought his heels to rest again on her desk. Locking his hands behind his head he said, "Your buddy Todd has been talking to people about running against Buster. I guess you know that."

"It's partly because of me, actually. I encouraged him. I just think we need someone other than a great first baseman to lead the town."

"You're not alone. I was part of the delegation that approached Buster, but I more or less went along for the ride. Come to find out most of the others did the same. His promise to discuss some issues 'possibly by election day' hasn't sat too well with folks."

"As a politician, Buster has a lot to learn."

"You think Todd Melville would make a good mayor?"

"I can't decide. He seems to have the interest, and he says he has the money."

"The word on the street is that you and he are an item."

Fran blushed. "Not true. We've been to dinner, and I think he would like for the relationship to be more than is, if you get my meaning."

"Loud and clear, Frannie. And I'm relieved to hear it."

"Relieved? Why?"

"I just wouldn't want to see you hurt."

"I'm a big girl. Besides, he's just a friend looking for some companionship. It's common after divorce."

Ed folded his arms across his chest and stared at her with renewed intensity. "Well, that's just it. Because some of the boys have started looking for a horse to ride other than Buster, they did some checking on ole' Todd. His wife in Dallas, Nan Tucker I think her name is, is not his ex-wife."

Fran emitted a low whistle. "Still married?"

"Correctomente. As a skirt-chaser, he's worse than me. Surprised?"

"Oh, just a little."

"Which means that the wheels have come off the Todd Melville bandwagon before the paint is dry on the 'Todd for mayor' signs."

"To say the least."

"Which also means that we have no alternative to Buster unless you run."

152

"Me?"

"Why not? A lot of people know your name from your editorials. Even the boys at the club are impressed, and they're not an easy bunch to get cozy with if you're a woman talking issues. I think I can raise all the money you'll need."

"What about the paper?"

"Being mayor of Centerfield is hardly a full time job. Besides, I'll hire an assistant for you."

"What's happened to the penny-pinching owner I've come to know and love; the guy who fought the health insurance war?"

A wry smile spread across Ed's lips. "Worse things could happen to this newspaper than you being elected mayor. Let's just say we can look for a little spike in our ad and circulation revenues."

"Can I interview and hire the assistant?"

"Anybody you want. You interested?"

She nodded mechanically, her mind elsewhere. "I'll have to think about it. Talk with the kids. But I have this strange feeling I may do it."

"Well, you don't have long, because we figure you'll need to make an announcement soon, before people get committed. The festival next weekend would be ideal." He sat up as if to leave. "Getting close to tee time."

"I'll let you know Monday morning."

"Works for me."

Chapter 58

Ed, Rick, and Jack Putt Out

Rick Lopez hung up the telephone, then shuffled his feet under his desk in the kind of brief and spasmodic victory jig a busy lawyer might permit himself. Fishburn himself hadn't been on the call, of course; that was too much to hope for. He had designated some underling to place the call initiating settlement. No matter. Rick would go nose to nose with Fishburn soon enough. He started to place a call to Ed, then realized he would be seeing him on the golf course that afternoon. Rick had taken up golf for client relations and played poorly once a week.

He waited until they were putting on the third green to bring up Fishburn. Rick mimicked the high-pitched, oleaginous voice of Fishburn's surrogate. "Mr. Fishburn recommends we start the negotiations in the fifty million range." I told this flunkie, "Perhaps Mr. Fishburn has momentarily, under the stress of counting all his money, forgotten what the judge said about this case. Your starting figure is about fifty million above what we had in mind."

Ed walked to the far side of the cup to align his putt. "I'm not paying a dime. Zero."

"You won't have to," said Rick. "I spoke with Wall-More's general counsel this morning. They smell a business opportunity amidst the stench of this lawsuit. They deal with the Fishburn's of the world on a regular basis. Cost of doing business, that sort of thing. They're willing to put up some settlement money provided they can pay it in gift certificates."

"Why would they be willing to pay anything?" Ed suspended his putter in mid-air to further refine his path to the cup.

Rick said, "Because it doesn't cost them anything. In fact, they make money. With their margins, a gift certificate is worth only a fraction of its face value, and they have plenty of research to show what else people buy, at full retail, when they come to redeem the certificates."

Ed, bent over his ball, putter in hand, shook his head without looking up, then sank a twelve foot putt. He winked at Lopez, retrieved his ball, and replaced the putter in his bag, where he stooped, unzipped a side compartment, and withdrew an amber bottle. "You mind if my friend Jack Daniels joins us for this round?" Without waiting for Rick's foregone consent, he stood, uncapped the bottle, brought it to his lips, and turned it up. His Adam's apple quivered. "Rick, whenever I'm tempted to condemn myself for being the idle, self-indulgent man I am, I think about times like this, when the sun is shining and the putts are falling and the whiskey's mellow and the night holds lots of promise and we've got some vermin like Fishbreath on the run, and I tell myself, I say, 'Ed, the good Lord put a whole bunch of serious people on this earth to do a whole lot of serious, worthwhile things, but you aren't one of them.' He wants me to do what I'm best at, which is this. I'm fulfilling my mission out here, Rick, keeping my date with Destiny and with Destiny's sister if she has one. I feel pretty goddamn holy at times like this." He grinned at Lopez. "Where are we going to meet Fishbreath to bridge this fifty million dollar gap?"

"We'll make him come to us."

"If we end up in your conference room, we'll add the rental to Fishburn's bill. I'm going to make that son-of-a-bitch regret the day he ever tried to squeeze me."

"He already does. And I'm thinking we may have a golden chance to stick the needle in a little further."

Ed approached, put one arm around Rick's shoulder as he held the bottle in the other, and began walking toward the path to the next tee. "My boy, that's an idea I want to hear all about."

155

Chapter 59

What Health Care Crisis?

Fran checked her messages upon her arrival at the *Sentinel*. The one on top instructed her to return a call to "Adriana at Big Toe HMO – "important." Whether from curiosity or disbelief, she dialed the number noted.

"I have very good news," Adriana reported.

"How long have you been employed there?" Fran asked.

"This is my second day."

"I thought so. What is the good news?"

"Dr. Punjabi wanted to let you know that the Senior Review Committee has granted your appeal and has therefore approved the throat culture for your son. The only condition is that you must bring him here, to our facility."

Fran sighed. "I don't want to be rude, and you obviously are too new to know any of this, but it was my daughter, it was months ago, and I didn't appeal. In fact, I no longer belong to the Big Toe HMO because I was fortunate enough to acquire real insurance, no offense."

"Does Dr. Punjabi know that you are no longer with us?"

"I don't know. I informed the last caller—I think her name was Rosetta—that I had made other arrangements. I have no idea whether she informed Dr. Punjabi, with whom I spent an entire fifteen minutes during my unfortunate tenure with your company."

"I'm sure he does not know."

"If he's there now I'll inform him. This has got to end." Fran said.

"Unfortunately, he is in India on vacation. He left me this note. I've never met him."

"Write this down," Fran instructed. "No more appeals, no more contact, no more Big Toe HMO. You have it?"

"I'll make sure he gets this immediately upon his return. Does this mean you won't be bringing your son in?"

156

Fran quietly replaced the receiver. She answered a knock at her door. Kirstin stood on the other side.

"Come in," Fran said, "you're right on time."

Fran would normally have taken a chair beside Kirstin as she disliked the physical and psychological barrier a desk represented, but this was a job interview and Fran was determined to approach it as such. She noted Kirstin's professional dress.

"How are things?" Fran wanted to know.

"My grades are great, my parents have been better, everything would be perfect if I could shake Pete."

"Still stalking you?"

"He follows me everywhere. He never approaches me or gets in my face. He's just . . . there. Always. Tomorrow I'm meeting with the college's security people to file a complaint. Once they bar him from the campus he'll risk a trespass arrest if he's caught hiding out in that stupid blue truck."

"Does he wait for you every day?"

"Rain or shine."

"I have a plan," Fran said, leaning forward to rest her elbows on her desk. "What time does your last class end tomorrow?"

"Seven-forty-five."

"Good. Still daylight."

"So?"

"So tomorrow when you come out of class you'll be met by a man. He's tall, very good looking, and single. Introduce yourself and take your usual route from class. When you get to the front steps where you can always see the blue truck, pause for a minute. Make sure Pete gets a good eyeball full of your companion."

"If this is a blind date, it's the strangest one I've ever had."

"It's a blind date with a purpose. If you two get along, whatever happens will happen, but I promise you that Pete will suddenly find better things to do at night."

"Who is the mystery man?"

"His name is Jeff Hanson. He's Pete's parole officer."

Kirstin's eyes widened. "He never mentioned having a parole officer."

157

Fran raised her eyebrows. "Imagine that. A man who didn't tell you everything. Remind me to introduce you to my friend Todd Melville. I can see we're going to have to work on your cynicism if you expect to make it in the newspaper business."

"Do you think I have a real shot at getting this job?"

"At the risk of beginning the interview at the end, you're the only candidate."

Kirstin folded her hands in her lap, hunched her shoulders forward, and suddenly looked quite vulnerable. "Why?"

"Because I want you. Your skills are marginal, but they'll improve. You have an excellent mind and I've watched you mature since . . . we met. I think you can do this work."

"This isn't a handout, is it? Did my parents have anything to do with it?"

"You know me better than that. It's a very responsible position. You're the first one outside my children to know this, but I've been asked to run for mayor and I've decided to go for it. I need someone here who can help keep me and the *Sentinel* together during the campaign and thereafter."

They spent the next forty-five minutes discussing Kirstin's duties as assistant to the associate editor. Fran gave her three research assignments, including one related to a follow-up Mid-East editorial Fran contemplated. Fran showed her the desk where she would work.

"Does the job depend on whether you're elected?" Kirstin wanted to know.

"Not at all. I've needed someone in here for the last six months."

"Is there anything else I should know before I start?"

Fran thought. "Yes. Ed, our boss, is going to hit on you. If he asks you to ride out to the golf course with him, tell him no. If he asks if you would like to see his putter, tell him hell no. Just let him know you're not interested. He'll be harmless after that."

Chapter 60

Na-Na-Na-Na, Na-Na-Na-Na,
Hey-Hey-Hey, Goodbye

Judge Frank gaveled the courtroom to order. Peering over his half-rims, he said purposefully to Rick Lopez, "Mr. Lopez, do you have good news for me today?"

Lopez glanced at a morose Arthur Fishburn before announcing cheerfully, "Judge, I'm happy to report that the parties have agreed on an amount. The form of payment, and its distribution, are still in dispute."

"Then, if I'm hearing you correctly, we have no settlement. Is that the case, Mr. Fishburn?"

Fishburn rose slowly to his feet. "Your honor, I cannot accept the terms proposed by the defendants."

"I can't force you to settle, Mr. Fishburn. Shall we revisit the defendants' motion to dismiss?"

"No," Fishburn virtually yelled. "I was hoping the court would intercede now that the amount of the settlement has been agreed to."

"Your Honor," interrupted Lopez, "if we're going to get into specifics I'd like my client present. She's outside."

Judge Frank nodded, then instructed the bailiff to announce the case in the hallway. As those in the courtroom remained silent, the bailiff went to the door and called out in a voice appropriate for summonsing a distant tribe, "All those having business in *Fifty-Thousand Tanyas v. Wall-More* step inside the courtroom, please."

Lucille appeared first, wearing her Wall-More greeters vest and a button with a smiley face. She was followed by another greeter, about Lucille's age, then another. As Judge Frank watched and Rick Lopez shuffled papers in front of him, the parade continued. They filed to the front of the courtroom and took seats.

Fishburn stood again, violently this time. "Your Honor, this is outrageous. I move these people be ordered from the courtroom."

Frank smiled at Lopez. "Mr. Lopez, who are all these good folks?"

"Your Honor, they are all employees of the defendant Wall-More with an interest in the outcome of the litigation."

"I see nothing wrong with their presence, Mr. Fishburn. The court instructs those who have just entered the courtroom to remain silent during the proceedings. Anyone who violates this order is subject to contempt. Is that understood?" In unison the two hundred greeters, men and women, nodded their snowy collective heads. "Proceed, counsel."

Lopez spoke. "Your Honor, the defendants have tendered an offer that we think is eminently reasonable in light of the highly questionable merits of this lawsuit. We have offered each of the plaintiffs a twenty dollar gift certificate redeemable at Wall-More. The value of the offer exceeds $1.2 million dollars based upon an estimated class of sixty thousand Tanyas."

Judge Frank nodded judicially. "What's wrong with that, Mr. Fishburn?"

"Well, Judge, the defendants have refused to make any provision for the plaintiffs' attorneys' fees."

"Oh, I see," said Judge Frank. "How much have they offered you?"

"That's just it, sir. Zero. Absolutely nothing for months of hard work by my law firm. As the court well knows, paying attorneys' fees is standard practice in this kind of litigation."

"The court is aware of certain common practices," Judge Frank conceded. "Tell me, Mr. Fishburn, from the pool of $1.2 million available to the plaintiffs, how much do you think should go to your firm?"

Fishburn stuttered momentarily. "Naturally, we think attorneys' fees should be paid over and above what they are offering my clients—"

"Yes, of course, but I hear Mr. Lopez saying they're not going to do it. Is that what I hear you saying, Mr. Lopez?"

Lopez stood. "Our offer is $1.2 million total, Judge."

160

"You see, Mr. Fishburn? It's all well and good if they'll pay your fees, but they say they won't. So, I repeat my question: from the pool of $1.2 million available to the plaintiffs, how much do you think should go to your firm?"

"At least . . . $1.1 million, Your Honor."

The judge shook his head slowly. "Oh, Mr. Fishburn. Surely each Tanya deserves more than a buck from a settlement in excess of $1 million dollars, don't you agree?"

"But Judge, you said yourself that attorneys' fees were standard practice—"

Frank's voice grew stern and impatient. "Mr. Fishburn, you brought a novel cause of action against these people, and I'm going to employ some novel relief. I'll approve a settlement providing for zero attorneys' fees. However, I cannot force such a settlement upon you. If you don't want their deal, say so and we'll hear argument on their motion to dismiss. What's your pleasure? What's that, Mr. Fishburn? I didn't hear you."

"I said we'll take it," Fishburn said.

Rick Lopez shook hands with Ed Abernathy, then turned his head to the audience and nodded faintly at Lucille. He began packing his briefcase.

"In that case, gentlemen, please prepare the appropriate order for my signature. Is there anything else?"

Fishburn spoke. "Yes, Your Honor. I know they're going to wave. Will the court instruct them not to wave?"

Judge Frank gazed gravely over the uniformed senior audience. "I instructed them to be silent and they have been silent. I see no need for further instruction." With that, he arose, walked off the bench, entered his chambers and closed the door just before exploding in laughter. He knew without looking what was taking place in his courtroom.

Chapter 61

Art Gets help from the Formerly Helpless

At her new desk at her new job, Kirstin felt she had entered upon a life that, if not new, was a euphoric departure from the old. Pete? Gone. Manicure? History. Easy sex? Not happening. The word "like"? Like almost gone. She greeted her co-workers in pie-eyed congeniality. In her new and parallel universe, the *Sentinel* offices might as well have been the navigation deck of the Starship Enterprise. She tore into Fran's three research assignments with the relish of, well, a woman who has never done serious work but discovers she likes doing it. With the new job came new statements of independence, such as making her own tuna fish sandwiches to eat at her desk so she could continue reading, and offering to pay George and Joyce rent from her first paycheck. Were it possible to measure self-esteem on a thermometer, her temperature was heading north toward normal.

On day three of Kirstin's new career, Art and Tricksy appeared at the *Sentinel* offices to keep an appointment scheduled with Fran by phone. Word had spread that Fran would soon be announcing her candidacy for mayor, and Art was determined to be on good terms with anyone who was or could be in a position to help New I.

Upon introductions, Fran's attention immediately went to Tricksy, as would be expected when an associate editor greets a woman who dresses for a business meeting in a rhinestoned silk blouse with a neckline that plunges to within two inches of her navel, and whose hair appears to have been teased by holding a fork in a light socket.

When they were seated in Fran's office, Art provided a brief history of his time in Centerfield and mentioned that because he expected to be a significant landowner ("several thousand acres"), he wanted to know more about the people who ran things, one of those "things" being the newspaper. Fran pressed him for details on

his use for the land, but he deflected her with "uncertain." Tricksy
chimed in that one use would most assuredly include building her
"the biggest goddamn hacienda in all of south Texas, with a hot tub
big enough to hold ten couples 'necked.'"

Fran folded her hands on her desk and asked if there was
anything the *Sentinel* could do to facilitate Art's transition to
Centerfield.

"Oh, yes," he said. "I'm interested in a tract of land that
adjoins one I expect to own, but I can't find the owner to negotiate."

Fran said, "Sounds like a good research project for a young
woman who works with us." She sent for Kirstin, who shook hands
when introduced and whose eyes widened discernibly when
assuring Tricksy that it was indeed nice to meet her as well.

"Perhaps," Fran said, "you can give us some background
that will allow us to help."

Art described the 10,000 acres ("sagebrush, cactus,
landlocked — nothing of value") and his efforts to trace the Porkrind
Trust. "I want to give them a fair price, but it takes two to twist," by
which he meant two to tango but he was still wrestling with some
American colloquialisms. He told them that landowners who had
acquired their titles through the Porkrind Trust had all dealt with a
man named Joe West from Laredo, who had died tragically five
years before when he choked on a chicken bone at a Baylor tailgate
party (compounding the tragedy, Baylor lost that day), and that a
Pan-American search for Joe West's records had turned up nothing,
nada, zilch. Art said he had heard zero from P.R. O'Kelly, the Dallas
registered agent for the Trust. Kirstin, taking notes, scribbled down
such addresses and phone numbers as Art had managed to collect.

"Let us see what we can come up with," Fran said. "Kirstin
will do some investigative reporting. If and when we solve this
mystery, she can write the story."

As Kirstin nodded, a certain confidence in the tilt of her
head, Fran focused on her transformation. "She can go anywhere,"
Fran told herself, and as if listening to a half-forgotten melody of a
song played at Fran's junior prom in the year she was the
homecoming queen, she heard the melody of her own life when all
things seemed possible.

Chapter 62

Fran Becomes a Politician as Ed Becomes a Statesman

On Sunday, a record 239 aspirants to the Bustamonte Barbeque Prize fired up grills in the pre-dawn coolness of what promised to be a perfect day for a festival. An aroma of mesquite floated on gentle winds from the southwest as contestants stood watch, sipping coffee or, in some cases, imbibing a hair of the dog that had bitten them in the hind end the night before.

Friday night's kickoff to the festival had deviated from prior years in one significant respect. As usual, Buster had appeared on the balcony of the town hall, doffed his baseball cap, and shot into the air the ancient revolver his great-great-grandfather had fired in the service of Santa Anna. Then, instead of waving goodbye to the crowd until the following day, he had signaled for quiet, withdrawn from his coat pocket a single sheet of paper, cleared his throat, and announced himself as a candidate for mayor, to thunderous applause. He committed himself to being "a good mayor," promised to do "good things" if elected, and seemed to make eye contact with everyone in attendance when he asked for their vote. On Saturday, after the traditional pilgrimage to Buster's hacienda following the parade, he had shaken hands with marchers and supporters, again asking for their support and waiving his usual fee for autographs.

Today, as the sun rose in a cloudless sky, fireworks erupted just off the town square. Contestants banked their fires to condition them for the meat, which in some cases had been marinating for a week.

At home, Fran heard the fireworks through her open bedroom window. She arose, made coffee, and read a chapter from *The Moralist*, a recent novel about a woman who runs for mayor of a small Texas town. She resisted the urge to skip ahead several chapters, preferring not to know if the woman got elected. At nine, she drifted back into sleep, awoke again, and walked down the hall to rouse James, Chip and Sarah. She fixed breakfast, showered, and asked herself for the twenty-first time if she had lost her mind.

At just after 1 p.m., to a large crowd gathered in front of the podium, Ed introduced Fran as the "next mayor of our town." As she stood at the dais looking out, she spotted Kirstin, smiling and waving with one hand while the other held the hand of Jeff Hanson. A few rows beyond them, she saw George and Joyce, who also waved. Among the hundreds gathered she saw other faces, less familiar but familiar none the less, and she felt at that moment less vulnerable to the popularity of the great Buster. Over the crowd wafted an aroma of pork, done to a pungent perfection by grill masters from the entire state.

She would compete for every vote, she told herself and them as she began to speak. She said she approached the election with the humility appropriate to a public trust, that she had some specific goals for the town if elected, and that she would need more help from them than they were used to being called upon to give. She promised to work for a child protection unit, to maintain a volunteer fire department, to resist any effort by a large, unnamed city to annex the town, to improve trash collection, and to hold the line on tax increases. She reminded them that they were all part of a great experiment called democracy, that America was still a place and an ideal worth fighting to preserve, and that at their core, American values offered the best hope for a better world.

Ed congratulated her, Chip and Sarah hugged her, and a steady stream of well-wishers promised help in the coming weeks. Ed had just taken her elbow to guide her toward an influential golfing buddy when he was approached by the festival chairman.

"Brock Rutledge is a no-show," the chairman reported, practically whispered, his angst palpable. "His flight is grounded in Oklahoma City because of some mechanical problem."

For the first and only time, Fran saw panic in Ed's reaction. "What will we do?" he demanded in a matching whisper.

"The executive committee just met," the chairman said. "We'll let our two Texas judges decide, and hope they agree."

"And if they don't?" Ed had forgotten Fran's presence, his attention fully devoted to the chairman.

"We'll ask you to step in."

165

"Me?"

"You know as much about Texas barbeque as any man walking."

"To talk about it, yes. Judging is another matter. I don't think I'm up to it."

"Sure you are," said the chairman. "Besides, chances are the two we have will see eye to eye on the winner. As I recall, you said as much in one of your editorials."

"Let's hope so," said Ed, breathing normally again.

It was not to be. As Fran circulated, shook hands, introduced herself and her children, and courted voters, a major riff developed between the two Texas judges, Paul and Ralph. In hindsight, the chairman later admitted, the dispute was preordained when the committee invited one judge from El Paso and the other from Texarkana--both in Texas by the slimmest of margins but at extreme ends of the state. They didn't even share the same time zone.

"It's hopeless," moaned the chairman in the presence of Ed and the two disputants. "You're so far apart you might as well be from UT and A&M."

"I went to UT," said Paul.

"I went to A&M," said Ralph.

"Oh, God!" cried the chairman, "why me? Ed, you've got to decide."

Ed motioned to Paul to follow him behind a partition. "What have you got?"

Paul said, "I've got me a little spitfire of a recipe over at 43." He pointed his finger at his own chest. "This 'ol boy's pulled some pork in his time, and this may be the best ever. It's as sassy as a Dallas lap dancer."

"The Booty Barn?"

"That's the one."

Ed emitted a low whistle. "That's some sass, all right. Let me check it out."

Ed and Paul returned to where the chairman, Ralph, and others stood waiting. Ed motioned to Ralph and said, "Let's talk."

When they were out of earshot, Ed said, "Paul tells me he's got some kick-ass barbeque over at 43."

166

"That he does," agreed Ralph, nodding emphatically. "That he does."

"But not a winner?"

"A strong second. Don't get me wrong, I like my 'que with some rough and tumble in it same as the next man. Forty-three will put a hair or two on your chest, I'll own up to that."

"Paul mentioned a lap dancer in Dallas."

"Must be The Booty Barn."

Ed said, "What beats 43?"

"One-Oh-Eight." Ralph spoke with the authority of someone who has seen the Promised Land. "I can't describe it, really. You'll just have to go pull you some. I had a teacher in seventh grade. I loved her. Real pretty woman, she was. Used to wear some perfume that reminds me of 108. Not the same smell as perfume, mind you, but still . . ."

"I'll try it," promised Ed, wondering how he could resolve a conflict pitting a Dallas lap dancer against someone's grade school crush. He guided Ralph back to the others.

When the chairman and Ed had excused themselves to confer, the chairman said, "Well, Ed, what do you think?"

"No chance of working it out. They're both solid."

The chairman sighed. "I guess you'll have to make the call." He placed an avuncular hand on Ed's shoulder. "This is what it's all about, Ed. You're like the president—all the easy decisions are made before they hit your desk. But look at it this way. Things could be a lot worse. This decision could have been in the hands of someone from New Hampshire. Just go out there and do your best."

Ed breathed deeply, letting the air out through puffed cheeks. "Yep."

At the judges' tent, the chairman, Paul, Ralph and others on the committee watched as Ed approached the two finalists, side by side on a table and labeled simply "43" and "108". He pulled a piece of 43 from a rib, placed it in his mouth, and looked up, as if the answer would be written in the top of the tent. He chewed it slowly, discerningly, and when he had swallowed he said, "Lord Miss Sadie, that is some fine barbeque." He asked for a beer, took a swig to clear his palate, then pulled a piece from 108, repeating the ritual. As the meat settled on his tongue, he saw a beautiful woman in his mind's eye. It could be Ralph's teacher, he thought. He wiped his hands, took another swig from the longneck beer, and said, "I've got to go with 108. It's got something about it unlike any barbeque I've ever tasted."

The chairman clapped him on the back. "Good job, Ed. We've got us a winner."

Minutes later, the chairman stood at the same podium from which Fran had spoken, addressing a crowd just as large. When he announced the award, a farmer in bib overalls, stooped and very elderly, came forward. "You say 108?" the farmer asked. "That's mine."

As the crowd applauded, the chairman shook the farmer's hand and gave him the prize. The farmer smiled and waved. The skin on his face and neck, wrinkled from years in the Texas sun, gave him the appearance of a happy raisin. After the other contestants had come forward to offer congratulations, Ed approached the old man, introducing himself as a judge, but not as the decisive judge.

"That's a unique recipe," Ed said.

The old man said something Ed couldn't hear. He leaned closer.

"Secret ingredient," the old man said.

Ed nodded, knowing the ingredient, whatever it was, would die with the old man, or be passed on to a favored son or daughter. That was the way of the barbeque world.

"Don't you want to know what's in it?" the old man asked.

"If you'll tell me," Ed said.

"Might as well," the farmer said. "I ain't got too many contests left in me, if you know what I mean. Prune juice. Two tablespoons per pound."

"Well, kiss my cactus."

Chapter 63

Kirstin hits Big D and Does A 14 Hour U-Turn

Kirstin reviewed the notes she took during the meeting with Art. The most obvious place to start was P.R. O'Kelly, because at least he could be reached and he knew details about the trust, even if he wouldn't or couldn't reveal them. She decided to make the seven hour drive to Dallas on the assumption that O'Kelly would have a tougher time slamming a door than the receiver of a phone.

In the reception area of Hoover, Coolidge and Harding, she announced that she was there to see Mr. O'Kelly and that no, she didn't have an appointment. Informed by the male receptionist that O'Kelly was at lunch, she seated herself in luxurious leather, crossed her shapely legs, and thumbed through a month old copy of Texas Today. Lawyers and clients came and went. Eventually, and older man with white hair and a Stetson approached the receptionist, who handed him some messages and then nodded toward Kirstin. The older man glanced briefly in Kirstin's direction, then looked back, measuring her up and down as he approached.

"Howdy, Miss," he said, extending his hand. "P.R. O'Kelly at your service. Won't you come back to my office?"

Kirstin followed him down a hallway lined with photographs of football players all flashing the "hook 'em horns" symbol of Texas football. At a corner office he paused to allow her to enter first. He directed her to a sitting area in front of a flagstone fireplace. When they were seated and she had briefed him on the purpose of her visit, he picked up the phone on the coffee table and asked that the Porkrind file be brought in.

"This is coming back to me now," O'Kelly said as he leafed through the file. Some guy named Art called a few weeks back. I told him I'd contact my client, and I did. Letter's right here in the file. That was about a month ago. No word from the client."

"Art has more or less given up," Kirstin said. "He came to my paper to see if we could pick up a trail that he seems to have lost." She mentioned Joe West.

"I knew West," O'Kelly said, shaking his head. "Sad, sad. Chicken bone, Baylor blowing a fourth quarter lead . . . it was almost too much."

"I don't suppose you can share the name of the client."

"Would if I could," O'Kelly said, closing the file. "The Porkrind Trust is about as secretive as any client this 'ol boy has represented. I've had firm instructions to keep everything confidential."

Kirstin pouted her prettiest pout, which seemed to encourage O'Kelly to say more.

"I can tell you that there has been very little activity on this file in many months — several years in fact. If the Trust was active, it wasn't active with us. We've been doing nothing more than the bare minimum to keep the legal entity in good standing with the state. If they've been selling land or developing, they've been using another firm."

Kirstin consulted her notes. "They sold a big parcel two years ago. The last piece, ten thousand acres, is the one I'm interested in."

"Here's an idea," O'Kelly said. "If I were you I'd trot on down to the courthouse to look at that deed two years back. Someone had to sign for the Trust. It may be the person I wrote to last month, or it could be someone else. Track down that person and I'd bet you my pet armadillo that you'll be in touch with the Trust."

Kirstin stood, reached for his extended hand, and thanked him for his help. As she shook his hand, she noticed his nails, cut close but well maintained. That was the sole relic of her manicure days, and she couldn't have been happier.

Chapter 64

Buster and George Take it Into Extra Innings

George and Joyce decided to throw a fund raising party for Fran. The addition complete, they saw a chance to exhibit their enhanced prosperity, to impress some of George's future customers, and to write off the entire event to advertising.

Selecting a suitable date proved difficult. Baseball season lingered, so all dates coinciding with Astros home games had to be avoided. A new football season was underway, meaning the schedules of the University of Houston, Rice, and the University of Texas had to be factored in. When at last they had identified a potential Friday in September, they ran a final cross-check against rodeos, tractor pulls, and wrestle-mania events.

Three hundred invitations went out. Joyce suggested they invite Buster. George reasoned that this could prove a bit awkward, as the one purpose not related to Fafalone Eternal Enterprises, LLC, was to raise money for Buster's opponent. Upon reflection, however, George agreed. Buster would undoubtedly be elected, and it would not behoove George or his business prospects to be on the wrong side of the final outcome.

"He won't come, of course," George said, "but at least we'll be on record as having invited him."

Virtually all invitees accepted, Buster included.

Joyce's excitement bordered on euphoria. "Just think, the great Buster is coming here, to our home."

In fact, Buster arrived early. He arrived first, to be precise, one half hour early. As his driver parked the limousine, Buster entered with his manager, his spokesman, his agent and a young nephew, who carried a large box. "Baseballs," Buster explained, suggesting to Joyce that a simple card table would be helpful. Within minutes, Buster took his seat at the table set up in the foyer, a pen in one hand, a beer placed to one side, and several baseballs arrayed in front of him.

Joyce and George greeted arriving guests, directed them toward the bars set up throughout the house, and then mentioned as casually as possible that the great Buster was, at that moment, seated just a few feet away, behind the crowd gathered at the table. The foyer soon became impassable, so that when Fran arrived at seven-fifteen, she could not get in. George spotted her, motioning her to a side door.

Fran took her diversion gracefully, having realized that the great Buster was akin to a force of nature. He could not be contained, therefore he must be accommodated. She entered smiling, shook hands with those she knew and didn't know, and passed out a single sheet of paper listing seventeen things she hoped to accomplish as mayor, written in English and Spanish.

Kirstin and Jeff arrived shortly thereafter. They had become a regular item after Fran's purposeful blind date arrangement. Minutes later, Kirstin approached Joyce.

"Mother, Buster is in our foyer."

"Yes, dear. Isn't it thrilling?"

"You invited him?"

"Of course."

"Fran's opponent?"

"Yes, he is."

"I know he is. That's my point."

"Your father said the same thing at first. But we must think of the business, too, and Fran really doesn't have much of chance, does she?"

"Not if Buster appears at all her fund raisers, she doesn't. Did the others here know Buster was coming?"

"Not unless they heard the rumor."

Kirstin sighed. "Well then, it's quite a turnout for Fran. At least that's positive. You've got to find a way to get Buster into another part of the house so Fran can give her talk."

"Why is that, dear?"

"Because I don't know what Fran intends to say. Suppose she criticizes Buster when he's standing right there."

"Oh, Fran wouldn't do that, would she?"

"Mother, it's a political campaign. That's what candidates do. Where is Scott?"

"He'll be along," Joyce said, looking over Kirstin's shoulder to track the crowd. "He had to work late at the geriatrics unit. He's so dedicated."

Kirstin turned to Jeff. "Maybe you could talk UT football with Buster. Take him to the Irish Pub for some guy-bonding type of thing."

Jeff brightened. "I can talk UT football with anyone."

Jeff recruited George, and together they persuaded Buster to move the autographing operation into the Irish Pub. None of them were present when Fran gave her short talk, welcoming everyone, thanking her host and hostess, the beaming Joyce, referring listeners to her printed position points, and asking for their help, monetary and otherwise. She did not criticize Buster, instead praising him as a valuable icon of the community. "I'm something less than an icon," she said, "but that might permit me to be something more of a mayor." This theme resonated, as shown by a collective nodding of heads.

Fran and Joyce had bid goodnight to the last of the attendees when Kirstin said, "Where are the men? They must still be in the Pub."

They arrived in the Pub to find Buster and George engaged in a serious game of darts. Jeff, Buster's driver, his manager, his spokesman, his agent and his nephew sat at the bar, having watched the game progress from the friendly match of earlier in the evening to the present testosterone-driven shootout. Alcohol-driven, as well, since both men had been drinking beer steadily for two hours. As their aim diminished, their intensity grew. Several of Buster's minions yawned and checked their watches.

Kirstin put her arm around Jeff's shoulders and drew him to her. "They look serious," she whispered.

Jeff nodded. "Yeah, we need to break this off before it gets ugly. You said to keep him occupied."

"You've done that," Kirstin agreed.

Jeff stood. "What say we make this the final game?" A chorus of "si, si" was heard along the bar.

Buster and George eyed each other in silent assent. "One last game," George said, retrieving his darts. "What shall we bet?" he asked, slurring his words and weaving noticeably.

173

Buster proposed, in an equally fuzzy argot, that if George won Buster would drop out of the race for mayor and that if he, Buster, won, George would hand over ownership of Fafalone Eternal Enterprises, LLC. When George said, "You're on," everyone except George and Buster knew that the final game was one too many. Jeff confiscated the darts as Buster's manager guided him toward the door, thanking the Fafalones over his shoulder as Buster's entourage made its exit. "Don't forget the baseballs," Buster could be heard to say.

Chapter 65

Kirstin Studies Tricksy's Dress Code

On her way back from Dallas to see P.R. O'Kelly, Kirstin wondered why, if the recorded deed to the last parcel transferred by the Porkrind Trust held a valuable clue, Art and Tricksy hadn't seized on it. On the morning she arrived at the courthouse record room, where Tricksy stood in full flower behind the counter, she thought it best not to ask. Tricksy greeted her warmly, coming from behind the counter to hug her. Tricksy wore a plaid mini-skirt, the first such skirt Kirstin had seen in years, a rattle skin belt with silver eyelets and clasp, and a sky-blue blouse knotted below her substantial kaboombas, thereby both lifting the kaboombas almost to Kirstin's eye level and exposing Tricksy's midriff. It occurred to Kirstin that Tricksy may have sought her fashion ideas in Hustler Magazine, of which Pete had been a faithful "reader."

"Are you on to something?" Tricksy wanted to know. "I can just smell that big hacienda Art's going to buy me when all this mess gets settled."

Kirstin related her trip to Dallas but omitted O'Kelly's suggestion, asking instead to see the recorded deed for the last Porkrind transfer.

"Sure enough," Tricksy said, leading her down an isle where heavy, dust-covered books were shelved. She picked one up and plopped it down on the counter, catching her left breast between book and counter. "Goddamnit," she yelled. "Third time this week. I got to remember to toss those books out further." She opened the book, riffed pages, then pointed to a deed. "That's it," she announced. "You have a look-see while I go find some Epsom salt to soak my tittie."

Kirstin, recovering her powers of speech, studied the deed. "The Porkrind Trust, party of the first part, hereby conveys unto Marshall Dillon and his wife, Kitty Dillon, parties of the second part, all that lot, piece or parcel of land being, lying and situate in

Buckco County, Texas, consisting of twenty-five thousand acres . . ." Kirstin fast-forwarded to the signature page, where above the grantor's attestation, she saw the name Monty Archer, Trustee. She made a note.

She left the record room and returned to find Tricksy, who was back behind the counter holding an ice compact to her left breast. "Damn thing's swelling up, if you can believe that," she said. "Any luck back there?"

"Maybe," Kirstin said. "If someone had wanted to change their name, where would they go?"

"Straight to court," Tricksy said. "Judge enters an order and that's that. Art did just that when he arrived. Course, the order gets recorded here, so it's legal and all."

"Can we check to see if a man named Monty Archer ever had a different name?"

"Sure," said Tricksy, "but I'm going to ask you to lift the book this time." She led Kirstin to another section of the record room. "Before 1950, that set of books there. After 1950 until 5 p.m. yesterday, this set here. Indexed by last name, either the old name or the new name. Let's check to see if this old boy is here."

Heads bent together, they ran down the "A" index. There it was: "Archer, Monty". Tricksy carefully turned to page 63, where they found a court order dated August 4, 1996, changing to Monty Archer the name of one Mamoud Abbar. Kirstin felt a tingle of discovery.

Tricksy said, "Well, Christ on a crutch, who wouldn't want a different name if his parents had stuck him with Mamoud. What the fuck kind of name is that anyway?"

Kirstin thought she knew.

Chapter 66

Fran Debates Buster, with Debatable Results

Fran challenged Buster to a debate. The consensus was that the great Buster, having what was perceived as an insurmountable lead, would decline, obeying the law of politics that counseled against giving dark horse opponents gratuitous exposure. But after a delay of some days, during which Buster's handlers checked potential conflicts with the baseball schedule, mall events at which Buster signed paraphernalia, a naturalization service at which Buster had been asked to swear in as US citizens a new crop of Korean immigrants, Fran was given exactly one date for the debate. Take it or leave it. She took it.

The event was held in the Centerfield High School gymnasium, where Mrs. Heckmon monitored the metal detector of those coming in. The crowd was standing room only. Seated in Fran's portion of the first row were Chip, James, Sarah, Kirstin and Ed. Seated in Buster's section was his wife and the five little Bustamontes. Buster won the coin toss and elected to speak first. To the applause of the crowd, he demonstrated his famous swoosh, almost knocking the microphone into left field. He thanked them for coming and for "electing me mayor." This brought a staff member dashing to the podium to remind Buster in a stage whisper that the election was technically still two weeks away. Buster's smile did not diminish in the slightest. He told the rapt and adoring audience that he wanted to give back to the community that had given him and his family so much, and that when elected he would do "good things," and he would avoid, at all costs, doing "bad things." No one could accuse the great Buster of getting off message, because his speech perfectly reflected his campaign theme, "Good things, Si! Bad Things, No!" For the last month bumper stickers had proliferated in Centerfield, reminding voters in red, white and blue letters that when it came to the issues confronting Centerfielders,

Buster's position was "Good things, Si! Bad Things, No!" With one more swoosh, Buster concluded his speech and sat down.

Fran rose. Polite applause greeted her. At the podium she waved to her family, then adjusted the microphone. "All citizens of Centerfield," she said, "join me in thanking Buster and his family for their contributions in making our town such a great place to live and work." Fran then staked out her belief that Centerfield could continue to rely on its wonderful volunteer fire department; that metal detectors in schools were an abomination; that more mental health treatment for indigents was a pressing priority; that another generation would be lost unless back to basics took hold in public schools; and that no society could call itself civilized without an adequately funded and professional child protection agency.

A question and answer period followed, during which Fran answered every question put to her by reporters from Houston media, and Buster apologized for having to take a phone call from the Commissioner of Baseball. In the far corner of the auditorium, a unified chant arose: "Good things, Si! Bad Things, No!"

Chapter 67

Art Imitates Life

Kirstin's research into the Porkrind Trust was, in a word, relentless. She saw this as her chance to justify Fran's confidence in giving her the job at the *Sentinel*. Through a contact of Jeff's at the Immigration Service, she learned that Mamoud Abbar had arrived in the U.S. in 1979 and had overstayed his six months tourist visa by thirty years. He listed his country of origin as The Gaza Strip, which in 1979 was no more a country than it was in 2009, but those were the days when the U.S. admitted essentially anyone who showed up on an airplane, when immigration and customs agents slept openly on the job, and when the Middle East was in such turmoil that no one knew or cared exactly where the The Gaza Strip was. Abbar paid $12 for a forged social security card with a number that had belonged to a man resting in an Austin cemetery for twenty years. He worked hard, saved his money, and eventually owned a chain of successful Hooters franchises.

Kirstin called one in Houston and was pleased to learn that Abbar was expected there the next day. Abbar had the complexion of tanned leather and a full shock of silver hair, although his eyebrows were pitch black and more or less ran the length of his forehead. When she introduced herself, he looked her up and down and assumed she was there for a job interview.

"No," she said, "I'm here to find out what I can about the Porkrind Trust."

Abbar's eyes narrowed. "You're from IRS?"

"No."

"Immigration?"

"No."

"SPCA?"

"No."

"Sierra Club?"

"No."

"Sam's Club?"

"No. I work for a newspaper in Centerfield."

"Which is where?"

"Bucko County. South of here."

Abbar nodded. "I know it, of course. The Trust once owned most of Bucko County and now it owns none of it."

Kirstin said, "You're sure it owns nothing now?"

"More or less," he said, shaking his head. A sadness came over his face. "If there is anything left, it can't be worth much. No oil. Lots of sand. I don't have time for it now that the dream is dead."

"And what dream is that?" she asked.

"Is this confidential?"

"No."

"The dream of New Palestine. Many decades ago our leader, Nosir Arrarat, may he rest in peace, had a dream of a country as far away from the Jews as we could get. He founded the Porkrind Trust to buy up land in Texas. But things became so bad in the West Bank and Gaza that we needed the money, so we had to sell the thousands and thousands of acres we owned. So we are left with only the very old dream of Old Palestine. It is very sad."

Back at the *Sentinel*, Fran emitted a low whistle when Kirstin revealed her findings. "The Palestinians thought they could establish a country in the middle of Texas? Now that is a news story, girlfriend. A first class job, which I will make sure Ed knows all about." Kirstin beamed.

Because the *Sentinel's* investigation had been spawned by Art's inquiry, Fran felt she owed him a report before the story broke. She reached him by phone at Tricksy's. From the copious weeping on Art's end, Fran concluded that her news was not what he had hoped to hear.

"So this is bad?" Fran asked.

"Bad? The Palestinians own a ten thousand acre tract in the middle of New I? It is utter disaster."

"What is New I?" she asked.

"I think I need to come see you," he said.

Chapter 68

Fran and Ed Look Forward

One week after the election, Fran and Ed sat on opposite sides of her desk at the *Sentinel*. Between them rested a couple of half-filled longneck bottles of beer.

Ed said, "Congratulations. You lost."

"Yep," said Fran. "But I gave him a run, did I not?"

"That you did. You surprised a lot of people, and I've already heard some chit chat at the golf course of putting you up again, maybe for the state legislature. You doing all right?"

"I was disappointed at first. It stings."

"Centerfield's loss is Centerfield's gain," Ed said. "You can do more for the town here than you could as mayor."

"Ed, for a guy who plays a lot of golf, you size some things up pretty well. That's what I've concluded, too. Newspapers are supposed to watch the government, not be the government." She paused, sipped her beer, then continued. "Maybe I'm just rationalizing defeat."

"I don't think so. Had you won, I would have been the only member for the Fourth Estate watching—if Buster had any sense he would have made that fact the focus of his campaign."

"He did all right just signing autographs."

"Tough to figure voters out. Here's how I look at it. If someone was a famous pilot, I'd vote for him to fly a plane. If she's a famous doctor, I'd second the motion to let her perform a difficult operation. But how do folks conclude that a baseball player can run a city?"

Fran grinned. "That's about as philosophical as I've ever heard you. Beats me, but the cult of celebrity runs deep in the good old U.S. of A. I mean, 'Good things, Si! Bad Things, No!?'"

"Speaking of celebrities, I didn't see Todd Melville at any rallies." He winked as Fran stuck out her tongue.

181

"I heard he took an extended cruise. I doubt he took his wife."

Ed leaned back, put the heels of his boots on the desk, and wondered where Fran saw herself five years down the road.

"Paying college tuitions," she said.

"We'll be a daily by then," Ed said, swigging his beer before resting it on his stomach. "You'll be our editor, of course, making a lot more money. Just think of all those juicy issues you'll get to write about. Why, I'll bet before it's over they'll bring you in to negotiate peace between what's his name and what's his face."

"Can you be any more specific?"

Ed flapped an extended hand to motion casually to some distant empire. "You know, Jerusalem. Those people."

"You mean Art Adams and Monty Archer?"

Ed nodded. "New I, New P. That whole headache."

"Actually, they have each asked me to help, so I'm meeting with them next week. The first order of business will be to let each of them know what a dim view Uncle Sam takes of any sovereign country on Texas soil."

"I guess they can confirm that with the Mexicans," Ed said. "So our own Frannie is going to be negotiating world peace? What next?"

She leaned forward, resting her elbows on the desk, Sphinx-like. "My son Chip passes through a metal detector every day at school. In a quiet little place like Centerfield, we screen our children for weapons before they are admitted. Think about that. These kids have just come from home, including my home, and the schools are saying, in effect, 'We can't be sure of what you're bringing to us from your parents, your family, or your neighborhood, and to protect ourselves and you we need to x-ray you.' Is that a price of a free society, or proof that we can't handle the freedom we have? Is it like a stop light, that simply makes traffic more orderly, or is it more like a border crossing, where suspicions run high and the guards are armed? Those school metal detectors worry me."

Ed stared at her. "Frannie, you're making my head hurt here."

"Sorry," she said. "I'm still campaigning and the election's over. Let's talk about you. Five years?"

Ed drained his beer with a satisfied slurp, then grinned like a schoolboy ready to push another, knowing that a friend had sneaked up on all fours behind him. "I was hoping you'd ask, because I want to show you something." He reached into his shirt pocket, withdrew a paper, and handed it to her.

Fran studied it, then him. "Ed's Barbeque Butter?"

"Yep. I'm going all the way with this."

She read from the paper she held. "A Texas Barbeque Sauce that's so good you'll want to slap your daddy." She frowned.

"It's an old expression where I come from—anything that grabs your notice in a really big way."

"You're going to market this?"

"Nationwide, Frannie. Remember a few months back when I had that offer to sell the paper, and I couldn't bring myself to do it? I said I needed something else in my life besides golf. Well, here it is. It's my destiny, don't you think?"

She slowly shook her head. "It just may be," she said, as much to herself as to him.

"Remember that old boy that won the barbeque prize last summer?"

"Unforgettable. He looked ninety."

"That's because he is ninety. I cut a deal with him. He gave me his recipe, including the secret ingredient."

"And he gets a share of the profits, I assume."

"Naw, he didn't want that. He's got enough money and he doesn't have any family left. You see that oval in the upper corner of the label?"

"Sure."

"His picture goes there. Not a current picture, but one he had taken when he was about forty. He says it captured him at the prime moment of his life."

"Wonder what happened."

"He wouldn't say. Just told me it was rare that a man had a picture taken at the prime moment of his life, and he wanted it on the sauce. Immortality, I guess. That's fine by me because it's a

183

good picture and he was a good looking man, rugged and all before age and the sun shriveled him up."

"Are you going to tell me the secret ingredient?" she asked.

"Are you going to sleep with me?"

"No."

They both laughed before Ed said, "Let's just say it's the enriched plutonium of the barbeque world. My lips are sealed."

"What if it doesn't sell? I think you need some market research on 'slap your daddy.' People in Minot, North Dakota or Newport News, Virginia have never heard that expression."

"They'll figure it out. And if they don't, it's their loss. See, Frannie? I've got my butter, and I've got my putter, and I've got my health, and I've got Texas — is this a great country or what?"

Fran grinned. "Makes me want to slap my daddy."

The End